GONE

A Thread of Stories

Books by Rumer Godden

Black Narcissus
Gypsy, Gypsy
Breakfast with the Nikolides
Take Three Tenses: A Fugue in Time
Thus Far and No Further
The River
A Candle for St. Jude
In Noah's Ark (poem)
A Breath of Air
Kingfishers Catch Fire
An Episode of Sparrows
Mooltiki: Stories and Poems from India
The Greengage Summer
China Court
The Battle of the Villa Fiorita
Two Under the Indian Sun
(with Jon Godden)
The Kitchen Madonna

Translated by Rumer Godden

Prayers from the Ark
and
The Creatures' Choir
(by Carmen Bernos de Gasztold)

GONE

A Thread of Stories

Rumer Godden

The Viking Press

NEW YORK

Published in 1968 by The Viking Press, Inc.
625 Madison Avenue, New York, N. Y. 10022

Library of Congress catalog card number: 68–16632

Printed in U.S.A. by H. Wolff Book Mfg. Co.

"The Little Fishes" and "Time Is a Stream"
originally appeared in *The New Yorker*. "Fireworks for Elspeth" originally appeared in *Woman's
Day* as "No Virtuoso"; reprinted by permission.
Certain of these stories first appeared in *Collier's,
Harper's Bazaar, Harper's, Ladies Home Journal,*
and *Tomorrow*.

Published in the United Kingdom and Canada
by Macmillan & Company and the Macmillan
Company of Canada under the title *Swans and
Turtles*.

Preface

🌱

I have named this small collection of short stories and sketches *Gone* because each is founded on a moment of experience, felt or seen or touched, that has long since gone, but that has left a small sediment or shape behind. Perhaps the book should properly have been called "grits"—though that reminds me of an American breakfast food—grits because every piece of writing, book or short story, play or poem, starts from what I call a "grit," something large or small, usually small, a sight or sound, a sentence or a happening that does not pass away leaving only a faint memory—if it leaves anything at all—but quite inexplicably lodges in the mind; imagination gets to work and secretes a deposit round this grit—"secretes" because this is usually an intensely secretive process—until it grows larger and larger and rounds into a whole. The result, of course, is seldom a pearl, but an author at work is like an oyster, clam-quiet and busy.

A name, a few words, can become a grit—perhaps end as the title of a book; a grit could be a glimpse, such as I had of the chef at the Pierrefonds beckoning that little lady. Sometimes a happening makes a story of itself, as with "To Uncle, with Love"; but even then it has to be given substance and shape: the smallest dust of anything can set it off, and there is no knowing how far or to what depth it will take you; the two words "Black Narcissus" grew into a novel and set me off on a lifetime of thought and reading.

Nor can one say why a particular "something" stays when thousands upon thousands simply pass by; why does "this" stay and not "that"? Wanting seems to have little to do with it. Often one tries to ignore the something or dislodge it, but a real writer knows there is only one way to do this—let the thing grow and then write it. Mysteriously, with most of us, once a thing is written, for the writer it ceases to have any interest at all.

One hopes this is only for the writer, that readers will find some sort of appeal in the stories collected here. There are gaps —for instance, almost all my stories with an Indian background have been published in the collection *Mooltiki*—nor are these consecutive in writing: some are early, some late. I have simply arranged them as they seem to go—and now, for me, they are gone.

RUMER GODDEN

Contents

🌷

GONE

A Thread of Stories

No More Indians

🌷

When I was small I was one of those children, so trying to their parents and themselves, who are a prey to nerves, imaginations, and nightmares. Almost the first thing I can remember is being taken to a fancy-dress party, dressed as Bo-Peep, but hardly anyone saw the pretty dress; I spent the party flat on the floor under a sofa because some big boys were dressed as bears, with bear masks. The story of the *Three Bears* was purgatory to me.

I was under my seat most of the time at pantomimes too; the Old Man of the Sea in *Sinbad* was especially terrifying. Jon, older by thirteen months and intrepid, poured scorn on me and must eventually have hardened me more or less; at nine years old and ten, I was playing the really horrible game we invented, Iurki, which was described in *Two Under the Indian Sun*:

> It was the game we chose to play when children came to tea in the cold weather. As soon as it was dark, we would inveigle them into the nursery where we would drag the heavy dressing-table across to one of the big wardrobes, put a chair on the table, a box on the chair, a stool on the box and everybody would climb up to the top

of the wardrobe, everybody but two—or one if that one were Jon. We huddled together on top of the wardrobe while the table-stool-box was dragged away so that we could not get down; then the lights were turned out and there followed a prickling silence.

It would be broken by a curdling scream perhaps, or moans, and a white-sheeted figure would come, twirling and shrieking at us. Or it might be a scratching at the foot of the wardrobe, and a voice wailing, "I'm dead-d and trying to come out of my gr-ave." Objects would be thrust among us; a chicken drumstick saved for the occasion, "My dead finger,"—it felt horribly like a long bony finger —or something round, squashy, warm, and wet was pushed at us: "It's my stump, the stump of my arm, blee-eeding. It's covered with bloo-ood." Soft things brushed our faces —it might be only a rag at the end of a fishing line, but it felt like a limp touch; worse was a hand in a stuffed glove or a knot of darning wool with loose ends, "A spider! A spider!" and a child was sure to shriek. Once a long slippery something that twisted and writhed as if it were alive fell among us with a hiss. "A cobra!" It was Azad Ali's hookah pipe, but even hardened Nancy let out a scream like a knife. It was a wonder one of us did not come hurtling off the wardrobe.

The game was to try and startle the children on the wardrobe into a cry or a shriek, when the frighteners would triumphantly call, "Iurki!"

Children used to beg their mothers not to let them come to tea with us. "Those dreadful little Goddens," said their mothers, and they used to telephone Mam . . .

Iurki gave me nightmares but I still played it: there was one terror, though, that I could not get over—and

still cannot come to terms with—a fear of Red Indians.
This is quite irrational because I have never seen a Red
Indian in the flesh—perhaps if I did, I should lose the
fear—but, shameful to say, they affect me as snakes affect
some people; even now I have only to go to a Western, a
thing I try never to do, and see the distant glint of silver
spear tips in the prairie grass—often the first indication of
a raid—or a spear with a tuft of feathers on it, stuck into
the side of a dead steer; or see an Indian Chief stand, fold
his arms and look into the camera, for the terror to start
up in me all over again. I instance films because it was
with a film that the fear began. Jon adored Red Indians
and when, for one of our father's leaves, we were in
England, and our mother, Mam, was in bed, having just
had our youngest sister, Rose, we prevailed on our nurse
to take us to *The Last of the Mohicans*. Jon must have
been, I think, egged on by our older cousin Kenneth,
because she was only six, I rising five, but we went, I
willy-nilly having to go too because there was nothing
else to do with me. The horror of those two hours is still
imprinted in me and was revived eighteen months later
when a well-meaning aunt took us, Jon and me, to the
White City where there was a rodeo and Red Indians
attacked a stockade. The aunt was kinder than our nurse;
this time I was allowed to come out.

It must have been this long ago planted terror that
made me write "No More Indians" because it is quite out
of character. Mick is a "fiction" child "made" as against
other children in my work who grew from a grit of reality;
but fiction or not, I have never felt a story more acutely.

No More Indians

❦   ❦   ❦

"An' I came round a great big bush, an' I almost bumped into a n'Indjun." The children, gathered round Mick on the back steps, drew closer. Three pairs of eyes widened, three mouths were tense. "What was he like, Micky? Tell! Tell what he was like."

"I'm tellin' you, Em'ly. Listen. Listen John n'Richard, only you mustn't let on or your pa will be at me for tellin' yous. He was big and tall and standin' very straight, straight as a tree; he was standin' by them red pines, and if he hadn't moved I'd never of seen him."

"Did he see you, Mick?"

"I'm tellin' you. He didn' see me."

"Can't be much of an Indian then," said John.

"Isn' he. You wait. I was bein' a hunter, creepn' from tree to tree. There's no one as quiet as me," Mick boasted. "He didn' see me but he wouldn' know I saw him. When he was still I had to look again an' again. Then I could see his face, dark and long an' it was wickeder and savager than the Indjuns in your books. He had black hair hangin' down, straight, as if it was cut outa' wood and painted, and his eyes! They moved like leaves do, catchin' the light. When they're still, they're dark."

"Mick, did he have fevvers? Did he?"

Mick hesitated. "Yes. He did. An' I thought that was queer. Indjuns don't have feathers these days 'less they're dressed up for folks to see. He had feathers all brown and black and white an' he had beads, all fancy. But he had a n'ax in his belt, same as they have in the pictures what's called a tommyhawk, an' it was all covered with blood. I think his hand was all bloody, too, but that may have been the light. As soon's I saw him," said Mick, his eyes getting rounder and bluer, staring over the children's heads, "I was skeert. I was more skeert 'n ever I been in my life. They'll tell you that all the Indjuns is way up on the Reserve, but don' you believe 'em. That there Indjun is walkin' round this very wood, prowlin' n' prowlin' around and I saw him. I couldn' move. I stood up and looked and looked s'if I was frozen. Then I went back, step by step, step by step. I dursn't turn my back on him, see? I looked at him all the time, and went back feelin' with my hands. Step by step—step by step—"

There was a piercing scream from Emily. She stood sobbing, her head in her pinafore. John and Richard looked startled and pale, shaken by her bloodcurdling scream. Mick's mother, Melindy, swept through the swing door.

"Mick Mohaghan, whatever have you been doin' to those children now?" She sighed and glanced fearfully at the study windows as she drew the weeping Emily into her arms. "You've been tellin' them tales again," she wailed. "Oh, Mick, can't you keep a hold on your tongue?"

"Here's Papa," said Richard, with satisfaction. "Emily, here's Papa."

It was the Senator, pen in hand, filling the whole swing door with his ponderous dark-clad body, frowning on them all over his beard, speaking out of another world. "What is the matter, Emily? Why are you making this noise?"

Emily timidly sniffed and Melindy offered, "She hurt herself, poor lamb."

"Kindly allow her to speak for herself. What is the matter, Emily?"

Emily gave a sob and a furtive glance at Mick.

"Well? I'm waiting, Emily."

"M—Micky . . ."

The Senator brought his gaze to bear on Micky. Mick looked up fearfully. "What have you been doing to upset Miss Emily?"

"I . . . I was tellin' about a n'Indjun I saw in the wood."

"An Indian?"

"Micky saw an Indjun, Papa, with a bloody tommyhawk. And he was all covered with fevvers."

"That's nonsense, Richard. Michael saw no such thing. There are no more Indians left in America except on the Reserve. And nowadays they go about in clothes like yours and mine. It's one of his tales again. He couldn't possibly have seen an Indian."

He looked firmly down on Micky, bearing him down; the blue eyes flickered, but Mick said, "I did."

"That's a lie. There are no more Indians. You tell these tales to frighten the children. You ought to be ashamed, a great boy like you."

Mick set his lip and stared stonily at the Senator.

"Say that after me, so that Miss Emily can hear you. 'There are no more Indians.' "

Mick was silent.

"I'm waiting, Michael."

"Micky!" It was Melindy's voice, pleading. He looked desperately at her, but her eyes were set on him in mute appeal over Emily's head. He turned away and looked over the stream to the wood, standing rich and red in the evening light. The light struck down through the trees, showing the still red forms standing sentinel, deeper and deeper into the forest; the ground was lost in a dense screen of bushes, thick and green with a mysterious light; they were still and secret under the trees, and then unaccountably they moved; waving, stirring, as if something had slipped between them. Mick smiled and looked up at the Senator. "No more Indians," he said.

It would have been easier for Melindy had Mick been a quieter sort of child, but he had the fatal, highly coloured, Irish boisterousness of his father and none of her native caution. It was hard in the 1900's small-town pettiness for the widow of the Irish ne'er-do-well to earn her living, and Mick made it harder. In spite of her slavery, Melindy was afraid to leave the Burgess house, and she was kept in continual trepidation by Mick's encounters with the Senator.

To his face they called him "Mister Burgess," but everywhere, behind his back, he was the Senator; his fine overbearing presence, his omnipotence, the way he had the strings of every concern in town in his hands, had given him the name. "And if he continues like this," they said of him, "we'll have to quit calling him Senator and let him just be God."

In his own house he was God. The whole family quailed before him: Melindy, drudging from dawn to dark, the sickly, fretful wife, the delicate, timid children. It was strange that so wonderful a man should have produced such ordinary children. Melindy thought that was the reason for much of his hardness toward Mick. He was jealous.

Mick had a peculiar quality about him, as noticeable as his faults. He had faults, glaring and Irish, not to be overlooked, as Melindy herself was the first to tell him, but for all his faults she would not have changed him; he was as extraordinary as if he had worn a halo round his head, and like a magnet, he attracted toward himself all manner of curious, unheard of, accidents and events. "Was there ever such a boy?" cried poor distracted Melindy. "You'll live to be hung, Mick Mohaghan. You'll never die in your bed."

And the worst of it was that she never could discover if these startling things were true or moonshine. Sometimes she thought he did not know himself. It was that that laid him open to the Senator; it was so fatally easy for Mick to fall into his tales, and then he was punished for a liar and threatened with expulsion.

"Oh, Micky, be more careful now," she would beg. "Try to behave right and proper if you can, boy, else I'll not be let keep you here."

He did try. He was useful. He helped his mother: he cleaned the shoes and carried water and kept her wood box filled. He helped Gene, the hired man, with the mare and the sorrel pony and milked the cow and ran messages and helped to mind the children. Those children were a mystery to Mick.

The house stood three miles from town, buried in the woods. The forest lay open to the house doors with only the stream between: miles of unexplored forest, combed with winding tracks among the trees; with glades and streams and strange tangled thickets; with a teeming life of tiny animals;

with hidden singing birds. Nearly all the trees were pines, and an enchanted pine smell came pungently from the tall red stems and from the ground that was thick with needles that hushed the tread; the branches spread a roof over the forest, showing the sky in patches and chinks, making a whispering sea noise as the wind blew.

Not one of the children had ever heard it until Mick told them about it; not one of the children had ever been alone in the wood. They were completely tame. Neatly and scrupulously dressed, they drove with their father every day to a private school in town, along the sandy road cut through the forest that hardly knew it at all; in the afternoons they drove back again. For the rest of the day they had their books and expensive toys, their visit to their mother's couch, their regular polite table meals.

Mick was a revelation to them. He walked barefoot through the woods to school and every moment he had, he slipped off in them. He came in for his food when he was hungry. He lived away, in the strange, forbidden, highly coloured world around their doors. He was not allowed to tell tales to the children, but fascinated, they would creep round him, and Mick could not resist an audience. Melindy thought they were beginning to live: they were becoming aware, conscious of the world touching them at all sides: they even developed small naughtinesses, but the Senator was not pleased.

"They are picking up bad ways from your son, Mrs. Mohaghan. I can't say I approve of the way in which you let him run wild. It's dangerous. Very dangerous."

Melindy opened her lips but only to say, "Perhaps you are right, sir."

"I know I am right." He stared at her. "You are his mother

and can't be expected to know any better. You need a man to deal with a boy like that. He must have discipline, Mrs. Mohaghan. Discipline."

She told Mick what the Senator had said. He was unrepentant. "You know what, Ma? I'd sooner die my way, than live the way he says."

"You'll be my death before you've done," she cried, but she kissed him as she passed.

She was still angry with him though, for frightening Emily with the Indian. He protested. "I did see him, Ma. Honest I did!"

"Now stop your lies, before I get Mr. Burgess to belt you."

"But I did see him," murmured Mick under his breath.

The next morning was hot. Very early there was a haze along the ground, soaking the grass and the heavy summer flowers; it lay thick in the woods, curling among the trees, which were smelling strong already. In his tattered blue overalls, Mick carried in buckets of extra water; they were too heavy for him and hurt his chest and arms, but he felt that made up to his mother for the trouble he had caused her last night. He brought in wood and sat down on the back step to clean the Senator's shoes. He hated to do it, but he hated more to see his mother cleaning them; he hated the fawning meek way she had with the Senator; it made him ashamed. "I shan't never give way to him like that," he boasted under his breath. "He shan't never worsen me."

"Are you gone crazy, sittin' whispering to yourself?" asked Melindy. She bent and put a package and a plate down beside him. "Here you are," she said, "and here's your wrapped dinner," and she put her finger to her lips at his cry of delight.

On the plate was chicken left over from the Burgess supper, and a mass of buttered potato and beans; the package held bread, a flour biscuit, and more chicken. "I'll tell them I made the chicken into soup for the children," said Melindy and stood there watching him eat, with a smile on her tired face. "Get off, else you'll be late," she said, taking the plate. He slipped the package in his pocket and took up his strap of books.

He avoided the road and went through the woods. Already it was very hot, there was not a breath of air under the trees. He went slower and slower, swinging his books by the strap; the early morning rising and his unaccustomed heavy break-fast made him drowsy. He blundered along, trudging in the thick, hot, green shade.

He stopped. He was suddenly wide awake. There was something close. There was danger. Something uncanny. He stood still on the path, tense, and slowly lowered his books to the ground.

He sniffed. It was a smell, coming from the thicket ahead. A curious penetrating smell that yet might not have been a smell at all, so unfamiliar was it. He did not know why, but it frightened him and made his body shrink into his clothes and his hairs separate themselves from his skin. He had seen an animal stand like that, a wild cat when it saw a dog, its stiffen-ing hair uprising at danger; and here he was doing the same thing. "Holy Mother of God!" he said silently, and as if that had made him a man again, he crept forward to the thicket and lifted the branches. An icy shock seemed to bolt his body to the ground.

Lying in the thicket was the body of a man, his blood spilled out on the pine needles. It was the smell of blood that had met

Mick on the path. The enclosed thicket was heavy with the smell. The man was lying face downward as if something had felled him from behind, and the blood was flowing from his back and head.

As he looked, with a sudden hot surprise Mick's good breakfast rose in his stomach and he was sick. For a minute that blotted out the man and the thicket; he retched and gulped and then, panic stricken at the noise he made, he fell on his knees under the bushes, holding his breath. He was giddy and faint and closed his eyes, trying to listen, hunching himself down; there was no sound, no movement, but the buzzing of the flies round the pool of blood.

He opened his eyes and forced them to look at the man. Then he saw, with a stab of surprised misery, that he knew him. No one else could have those moleskin breeches and the belt with the three graded knives, worn just behind the left hip where they could be drawn in a flash. Death must have been quick, to give Joseph Ducroix no time to draw; he was a half-breed Frenchman, a trapper and a hunter, and there were great tales of his prowess. Mick knew him in a gentler aspect. All summer long French Joe peddled goods from town to village to town, across the state. The Burgess house knew him well. He had often carried his pack into the yard and spread his things out along the porch, to amuse poor Mrs. Burgess. The children welcomed him for the funny way he talked and the different things he carried for them in his pack; now it lay, toppled ahead of him, untouched among the spindles, the same pack from which he had given Mick a knife with only one blade broken, and charged him nothing for it.

Could it be Peddler Joe? Mick crept forward on his knees

beside the body and laid a hand on it, starting from the touch of the moleskin breeches. They were still warm, as if Joe were asleep, not dead. Mick put out a trembling hand, careful not to touch the blood, and gently pulled the chin round; his fingers touched the beard and he snatched them away; they were sticky and wet with blood and frantically he wiped them on his breeches, rubbing them there long after they were clean. Then he saw what he had not seen before.

Turning Joe's head he had exposed the back. It was ragged, torn, with pieces of flesh and skin dangling. Joe had not only been knifed in the back. He had been scalped.

Mick was out of the thicket and tearing down the path, sobbing and screaming and crying as he ran for home.

The Senator was at breakfast. He sat at the head of the table, freshly washed, his linen shining against his well-brushed coat, his hair oiled, his beard combed; his feet, in the shoes that Mick had cleaned, were placed on a velvet footstool; he was attended on one side by Emily and John, on the other by Richard, while Melindy carried the dishes in from the kitchen.

There was a sudden scudding of bare feet, an uprising of dust as the door was flung open and Mick, dishevelled, white and breathless, fell against the table. He pushed past Richard and seized the Senator's arm. "Come . . . Come . . ." he panted, and choked over his words.

The coffee from the cup in the Senator's hand went over the cloth, over the snowy napkin, the plate of fried cakes, and dripped on the carpet in front of Emily, who stared at it with fascinated eyes and made no attempt to catch it. Part of it fell, hot and rich, on the Senator's trousers. Melindy made a noise between a cry and a groan and rushed to the kitchen for a dishcloth. The Senator's face had gone a curious mottled colour. He shook Mick off his arm with a cuff that sent him across the room.

Mick hit a chair and fell back over it, lying there, his arm up to shield his face. "Wait! Wait!" he cried. "Mr. Burgess, I got somethin' to tell you. Honest! Don't hit. Wait!"

"Well, what is it? I warn you if it's a tale—"

" 'Tisn't a tale. 'Tisn't. Mister, I found him in a thicket 'n the forest. It's Peddler Joe. You know. Summer he comes round sellin'. Joe. French Joe. I found him in the thicket. He's dead!"

"Dead?"

"Yes, sir. I found him. He's dead."

The silence made him look up. Slowly he rose from the chair and straightened himself. The Senator, his mother, even the children were looking at him, with stricken consternation on their faces. A flicker of excitement ran up him, a stirring of melodrama, and he said eagerly, "First thing was—I smelled blood. I was on the path, 'n suddenly I smelled it."

"How did you know it was blood?"

"I knew," Mick boasted. "I smelled it 'n I looked for it. There he was, lyin' face down in the spindles, and there was pools and pools of blood."

Emily ran to Melindy with a cry.

"But I didn' mind," cried Mike. "I went up to him and turned him over, 'n his face was all blood, too, and his eyes were starin' like this. . . ." He drew down his eyes with his fingers, and John gave a yelp of terror. "Then I looked at him closer 'n I saw . . ." his face paled and his eyes widened. "I saw what had happened to him. Mr. Burgess, he had been scalped."

There was an absolute silence. They were all looking at him.

"The Indjun had scalped him," said Mick.

There was a movement like a ripple across the face of his listeners; Melindy was gazing at him in an agony of reproach, Emily stopped crying, the boys watched their father; the Senator was wiping down his trousers.

"Very amusing, Michael," he said. "Very entertaining. You succeeded in frightening us all. I even believed you myself. It was very well done, my boy."

Mick stood aghast. "But it's true," he gasped. "Mister, it's true."

An uncomfortable small doubt uprose in his mind. "Perhaps not every word of it," he said. In a frantic effort to be honest, he went on. "I did put in little bits, maybe, to make it sound good. But I saw the Indjun, Mister Burgess. Honest I did, and he did—"

The Senator's hand seized him, pulling him up to the chair at the top of the table, holding him by his screwed-up shirt like a puppy by its scruff. "I think you've amused us enough, Michael Mohaghan. You're nothing but an inveterate little liar. You've frightened your mother and these children half out of their senses. Do you know what I'm going to do to you?"

Mick was very near the bearded face; he could feel the Senator's breath coming and going sharply by his ear.

"Do you? Answer me."

"N—no." His lips hardly opened.

"I'm going to ask you a question. Do you remember what you told me last night, in front of the children? 'There are no more Indians.' Did you see an Indian in the wood, Michael?"

"Yes." It fluttered out.

"And the Indian scalped French Joe?"

"Yes."

"You shameless little liar."

"I'm not a liar," breathed Mick.

"Aren't you?"

"S—sometimes. Not now."

"I think you are. I think very soon you'll tell me so yourself. I'm going to put you in the washhouse and I'm going to lock the door and take away the key. This afternoon when I come home, I'm going to ask you those questions again, and if you still think you saw the Indian, Michael, I'm afraid I shall have to beat you. There's only one way to cure you and that's to beat you. I shall be home about five o'clock: you have nearly all day to think it over. No dinner for him, Mrs. Mohaghan. Leave him alone until I come back."

"It's good of you, sir, to take so much trouble, but do you think . . ." quavered Melindy.

"It's my duty, Mrs. Mohaghan," said the Senator solemnly. "As I see it, it's my duty."

There was nothing in the washhouse but the copper and tubs, the old mangle, and a heap of clothes pegs; there was nothing to do and nothing to see; the only window was high up in the wall. Mick could tell how the morning went by the sunray which lay in a streak along the floor; as the sun went higher, the ray shortened. "By noon," he thought, "I reckon it'll be gone." He felt that ages of time had passed and still the ray was not half gone. He was feeling hollow and sick with misery and hate; the dry taste of his sickness lingered in his mouth and his eyes ached with his effort not to cry. He would not cry; and for all the beating in the world he would not say he had not seen the thing he knew he had.

Through the slit of the window, if he craned back against the far wall, he could see the tops of the near trees in the wood. He thought of French Joe lying in the thicket, hidden, and himself powerless to make them go and find him, or make them face the Indian. He was only a child. People would not listen to children. Even his mother had betrayed him; he would not think about that, but he seethed with hate as he thought of the Senator, and he gloated to think that he was wrong. "He thinks he's God A'mighty. He thinks he can't be wrong. But he is. He is, 'n he is!"

He heard a whisper from above him. "Mick. Mick."

It was his mother. She was miraculously looking down on him through the window, signalling to him to be quiet. "I got a ladder," she whispered. "See, can you get on the copper and catch my hands, and I'll try and draw you up. Sch! Don't make a noise or Mis' Burgess'll hear."

To climb on the copper was easy, but she had not the strength to pull him up. "Ma," he whispered, "pass your apron through the window. Undo the waist but don't take it off. You can take my weight on your shoulders and haul me up like that."

She did as he told her, bracing herself against the frame. The heavy sacking apron stood the strain, and he just managed to grasp the edge of the window. Like a cat he hauled himself to the sill.

"You go down," he said. "I'll follow."

It was a business to disengage her apron, and drag it back without upsetting him, but at last she was down and he followed her. She drew him out of sight behind the wall.

"I ain't got too much time," she said, "but this is somethin' I think ought to be done. I've been thinkin' it over, Mick. Seems to me you wouldn't have dared to do that, breakin' in on the Senator like that, for nothin'. I've been thinkin'—maybe he was wrong and you did see somethin'! I've told Mis' Burgess I'm out to get potatoes. Now Michael Mohaghan, you take me straight to where you say you saw Peddler Joe."

"Ma, you'd come!" he cried joyfully, then his eyes turned to the wood, hot and silent in the rising heat. He seemed to grow small with fear before her eyes. "Ma," he said, "I daren't."

" 'Cause it's all a lie?"

" 'Tisn', 'tisn', Ma," he begged her. " 'Tisn' no lie. But it's the Indjun. He done that to Joe. What if he catches us?"

"Very well," she said, closing her lips. "You're a liar and back in the washhouse you go."

"Ma!"

"I'd sooner see you scalped than a proven liar. And sooner be scalped myself than break my heart. Well, Mick, you can say which it's to be. Back into the washhouse or into the wood with me?"

His face was piteous, almost babyish as he stood trying to make up his mind, but she hardened her heart. "It's your only chance. If I say I've seen Peddler Joe dead, with my own eyes, they'll have to believe you, son."

Without a word he turned in front of her, and led the way across the bridge and into the forest.

There was a lowering oppressive stillness under the trees. Melindy caught it as soon as they entered the wood; her eyes darted this way and that as she followed Mick's small silent figure, and she could have sworn that something was moving with them among the still red pines. Under the trees the wood was open, but the light between their stems was tricky; it seemed to move and yet was still; they ended in dense green thickets where anyone could live for days, and opened into glades of tall grass that brushed around her skirts. They'd never find an Indian here, she thought, and looked sharply round. There was no sound, no air, only the sunlight filtering down through the red stems and the rank, still heaviness about them.

Mick stopped, with a whisper. "This is where I smelled the blood."

She sniffed, trying to smell it, too, but the smell of pine and undergrowth was overpowering in the heat.

"There, behind them leaves is where he is."

She looked fearfully at the tangle of bushes where he pointed. She could not believe; yet she believed. There, a few yards from her, screened by the leaves, lay the body of Peddler Joe, from whom she had bought her needles and thread, the actual stuff of the gown she was wearing. She trembled but still she could not believe it; then her foot hit against something hard, and looking down she saw schoolbooks where Mick had dropped them. That was not even in his tale; he had dropped them and left them unknowingly. He had been frightened as badly as that. She went forward and parted the leaves.

There was an intense stillness. Mick would not go nearer, he stood behind her waiting. He was in a fever for them to get away, but with a feeling of dignity he waited for her to turn to him and tell him that she was sorry.

"Mick, come here." Her voice was loud and clear and very angry.

"Take a look at that," she said.

He looked and blinked his eyes, and looked again. The thicket lay carpeted with leaves and spindles—empty.

"Did you see an Indian?"

"Yes."

"Did you see French Joe lying dead?"

"Yes."

"How did he die?"

"He was scalped."

"By the Indian?"

"Yes."

"You're sure?"

"Quite sure."

"In that case, Michael, I must beat you again."

In the hot evening the sound of the belt falling on Mick's back was magnified in the air. Melindy put her hands over her ears in the kitchen, watching the clock. "It's the devil that's in him," she moaned. "All this time and still he won't give in." The children huddled themselves outside the door; Emily wept and shuddered, the boys kept peeping in at the window to see how it was going.

"He won't give in," cried Richard. "He gets three belts every time."

"Oh, how can he be so wicked!" cried Emily. "Oh, how can Papa be so cruel!"

"He's not cruel, he's right," said John. "Mick tells such lies. He's got red stripes all down his back."

"Did you see an Indian?" The Senator was breathing hard. He was not relishing this. He tried to hit evenly, with a cool head, to put his questions in a cool, just tone, but Mick was wearing him down, and more curiously, he was filling him with self-disgust. That was a strange feeling for the Senator. It was not merely beating a naughty boy; it was like catching an animal that acted on instinct and trapping it and tormenting it. That was absurd. Then, why did he feel so much of a bully? He was giving an obstinate boy a well-deserved thrashing. He was no bully. Then why did these uncomfortable thoughts come crowding into his mind? He was on the edge of losing his temper. "I shall not lose my temper. I shall be just and temperate. I am just and temperate. I am doing my duty."

"Did you see an Indian?"

"Yes."

It had gone on for half an hour but the Senator and Mick had lost all sense of time. The sweat was pouring off the Senator's wrist, a band seemed to be pressing round his forehead, and he had giddy spots in front of his eyes. Sometimes he only saw Mick as something small and white, bending over a chair in the corner, or standing up to answer him; then he was startlingly clear, with a swollen, unrecognizable face from which blazed two hot blue eyes.

"He was scalped." The answer was shot back at him like an arrow and the eyes burned.

His breath came in gusts. "In—that—case—I'm afraid I must—beat you again."

He could hardly see the hoop of Mick's back over the chair. "I—must—not—hit—him—hard." He lifted the belt clumsily, not seeing where he aimed and brought it down smartly on his own leg. The surprising cut of it made him cry out. Mick looked round.

Richard cautiously raised himself to look in, outside the window, and stayed there transfixed by his father's face.

The Senator rushed down on Mick, and with hoarse broken noises like sobs, he slashed at him over the chair. He saw him drop to the floor and still he went on hitting. An effluvium, real, like blood, was in his eyes and nostrils choking his mouth; he had lost all sense and reason. Then he heard Mick's frantic crying and he dropped the belt and stumbled to his chair. Shuddering, he sat there, his hands over his eyes: from the floor came that broken, defeated crying.

"Did—you see an Indian?"

There was a pause. "N—no."

"Say it after me. 'There are . . . no more Indians.' "

"N . . . more . . . Indjuns."

"Now go."

On his hands and knees, Mick crept sobbing out of the door.

Melindy went out on the back porch and called into the shadows. There was no answer. All evening she had called and waited. She had gone out among the bushes, calling softly, peering under them. Now she sat down to wait, trying to pierce the darkness with her tired eyes, calling again. Even while she sat upright, looking anxiously into the night, from habit she began to rock. The sound carried to Mick where he lay in the grass by the fence; he had crawled there between consciousness and fainting, and lain in a daze, waking to cry a little now and then. He had heard his mother, but made no move to answer her, turning away from her with a bitter misery. Now the sound of the rocker came to him across the garden, reminding him of all the comfort he had ever known. It melted his heart; he began to cry like a baby and presently he crawled out from under the fence. The pain, as he stood upright, made him break into hysterical sobbing, and he almost ran across the grass to his mother's chair. "Ma! Oh, Ma! Oh, Ma!" he cried. "It hurts so bad."

She sprang and caught him, and felt him wince and shrink as she touched him. She drew him into the kitchen light; then as she saw his back and neck and hands she began to cry as brokenly as he, and all her suppressed hate broke out against the Senator. She would have gone for him then, but Mick clutched her, so weak he could hardly stand. She locked the kitchen door and fetched the Senator's own hip bath from the scullery and filled it with precious hot water. When she saw Mick glance at the door and bite his lip as the water touched him, she said fiercely, "Cry if you want, my lamb. Let him come, brutal great bully. My lamb! My poor lamb!"

But later when she had him wrapped in a blanket in her arms on the porch, he lifted his head from her shoulder and said, "Ma."

"What is it? My little son!"

"Ma, it don't make any difference. He can lam me ef he likes. I saw the Indjun."

She stiffened, pushed him off her lap. "I've said it's a devil that's in you, Mick, and I'm right. After all you've had, still there's wickedness in your heart, and on your tongue. Get out of my sight. I'm done with you."

The morning was Saturday. There was no school and Mick

was glad. For two days he could escape going into the wood and in two days perhaps something would happen to make them believe him. After his troubled, pain-filled night, when for the first time in his life he could not sleep, the wood seemed more sinister than ever. It seemed to crowd down on the stream and round the road and bridge, trespassing up to the very gate. The close pine stems seemed blood red in the light of the morning like shot arrows quivering in the ground. He was afraid even to look at them. His back was too sore to carry buckets that day, and it turned his heart sick to see his mother go down, close, to fetch the water from the stream; any minute she might look up to see the Indian watching her from the trees, ready to spring on her.

The children went down on the bridge to drop walnut shells for boats into the stream; it was he who had taught them to do that; now he wished he had left them as their tame little selves, content with the garden, away from the deadly brooding wood and the terror that lurked there among the trees.

He dared not say a word to anyone. He went through the day silently, his eyes on the ground, trying to escape notice.

In the afternoon the Senator called him. "Gene has gone to town," he said. They avoided looking at one another. "Are you too sore to ride?"

Mick flushed. "I'm not sore," he said scornfully. " 'Course I can ride."

"Saddle the pony then and take this note to Jules."

Mick paled. It was four miles to Jules and the way led through the forest.

"Afraid?" asked the Senator. "Of Indians perhaps, Michael?"

Mick held out his hand for the note.

They saw him disappear on the sorrel pony into the woods under the pines, riding swiftly and awkwardly with his sore back. Melindy watched him go and turned back to her work with a sigh.

At first he rode in a blind maze of terror, oblivious of his pain, quite numb with fear. As the sorrel went quietly along under the trees, his reason came back to him and then it was worse. He stared into the trees until his eyes ached; in front of him, behind, to either side; he could not look everywhere and he gripped his reins and rode as fast as he dared. That hurt him too much for endurance; the branches whipped against his tender sides, and every touch made him start with fright. He slowed down, and now it seemed to him that the pony's feet made a resounding noise on the path; he quivered at every sound, each breaking twig, and when a pigeon whirred out of the grass it nearly sent him out of the saddle.

It was impossible to go on being as frightened as that. Now he was coming to the glades, and in spite of the pain, he touched the sorrel with his heels, sending her forward. It was better. He could see farther now; there was at least no chance of a surprise.

But again they entered the close forest, a path between high bushes; the sorrel pricked her ears. He reined in and sat, crouched down, listening. The pony danced impatiently, snatching at her bit, fidgeting, crashing into the bushes. There was another glade in front of them; he could see the opening ahead and he let her go.

It was then that he dropped the note.

He saw it fall, making an arc in the air; he clutched at the streak of white as it dropped, and his heart seemed to tumble from his mouth. He had to get down and pick it up. He had to get down.

He held the pony, looking searchingly round the glade. It was not big, no more than a dell, bright with flowers, the forest coming down to a bank close around its edges. He listened. There was no sound but the sorrel's impatient snorting and a peculiar sound of pulsing like drumbeats in his ears. Holding firmly to the reins, he swung stiffly to the ground and bent down to get the note. The sorrel pulled away; he had to stand again and tug her back, wrenching her head to make her stand. Again he bent, and he picked up the letter. He stood up and saw the Indian.

He was standing on the bank, just above him. He might have been there all the time among the trees. He stood on the bank, his arms folded, looking down on Mick and the sorrel pony. He was not dressed as Mick had first seen him; he was nearly naked, with only a cloth and a belt round his waist. Mick's eyes fastened on that belt. It was Peddler Joe's; he could see the hilt of a knife shining on the dark hip, and the axe hung there too: and there was a strange small object hanging in front, something shrivelled, with black threads hanging down. At the sight of that, Mick's breath seemed to rise in his throat, choking him, and his eyes lifted irresistibly to the Indian's face.

The face was lit by a smile, a senseless grinning smile like a dead animal's when it does not feel any more; and his eyes were on Mick with the shifting light that he had seen in them before.

Then Mick began to step back towards the pony, keeping his eyes on the Indian. Just as he had told the children, he went back, step by step—step by step—as he had done in the story, but it was not a story now. Where Emily had given her scream the Indian sprang from the bank to the glade in one mad leap.

Into the quiet of the Burgess afternoon there rode a troop of men with guns and dogs shattering the stillness of the forest. They hailed the Senator from the bridge. "Burgess! Hey, Burgess!"

He came out onto the porch, looking down on them.

"Burgess. You'd best keep your wife and kids indoors. We're out for a mad Indian hiding in the woods. Two fellows have been trailing him west, and traced him here. We've got dogs on him now, and he's been round your place."

"An Indian?" The Senator was at the gate, stammering out words.

"He's dangerous. Thinks he's gone back to the ways of his people. He's on the warpath."

Another man pushed up with a grave face. "He got old Joseph Ducroix. The dogs found the body just now. Hidden in the bushes, and the place where he did it all, covered up with spindles. He had a try at scalping him too. . . . Any of you seen anything of him?"

One of the horses neighed. There was an answering whinny from the wood, and the sorrel pony stepped out into the road.

With ears pricked and gleaming unconcerned eyes she came toward them. There was a frozen silence as she came. The Senator stood gripping the gate, and from the house behind them rang out a woman's scream.

Mick was strapped, face upward, across the saddle. Blood

dripped from his head. The note was still in his hand and his lips were parted as if he were saying something into the sky.

The Senator heard. The lips, the forest, the red sunlight were saying into the stillness, "No more Indians."

❦

Down Under the Thames

🌷 and 🌷

The Little Fishes

In the days of our childhood English people living and working in the East—excepting those who were very poor or very wise—sent their children back to England to be brought up, even though this meant years of separation during which the children were exiles. We, Jon and Rumer, were two small English girls; India was where our father worked and we lived there until we were taken to our grandmother and maiden aunts in England. Then suddenly we were fetched back, reprieved for five years.

This is the opening of the autobiography that in 1966 I wrote with my sister Jon; she is Deborah in "Down Under the Thames," Ruth in "The Little Fishes" because these two short stories were, I suppose, forerunners of the book. They were written long before the autobiography but in actual time they are placed, the first before the five years of *Two Under the Indian Sun,* the second after them.

I had long wanted to write about those Indian childhood years and did this under the veil of fiction in a short book, *The River,* which afterwards was filmed in a memorable classic by Jean Renoir in 1949. *The River,* though, was not the end of that particular writing vein; it was still strong, and four years later I wrote "Down Under the Thames," but still as fiction; the house was my grandmother's, I was the small Alice and can still see that terrible willow-pattern pan with its dark opening; this has a direct link with the thunderbox club in *Two Under the Indian Sun*. (I am not obsessed with lavatorial details but there was undoubtedly a searing psycho-experience here.) I can see too, the tray cloth with its bloodstains from my pricked fingers; we used also to herringbone flannel dusters and make useless buttonholes on strips of linen; I have never willingly sewn or embroidered since, in fact I am shamefully clumsy with a needle.

After the publication of *Two Under the Indian Sun*, Jon and I had, and are still having, many letters asking what happened to us next? What happened, they ask, at the end of that five years in India when we came back to England? Did we go to school? "The Little Fishes" is in part the answer, though it was written long before the book.

Once again this story was written as fiction, perhaps rightly so because the ending is imaginary; Jon and I never settled at our school of St. Monica's as Ruth and her sister did in theirs, probably because ours was too physically rigorous for girls as delicate as we were then. Jon had malaria, of which the nuns had no experience; when her temperature jumped and then sank, as malaria temperatures do, sometimes up to 105°, two hours later below normal, they thought she had been rubbing the thermometer on the bedclothes—a school trick that we poor innocents had never even heard of. She was made to get up and was sent back from the infirmary into school, this on a day of ice and snow; but rescue was coming. Our mother became alarmed at the lack of letters—they were censored by the Sister Superior and our wails were not posted—and a friend was asked to call and see us. When she came, we were in class, and she was told we were not available; but the friend was Jon's adored and aristocratic Mrs. Fitzgibbon-Grey, who calmly replied that she would sit in the Sister Superior's office until we were available. When we were produced—as we speedily were—she was so shocked by our looks, especially Jon's, by our thinness, coughs, and our hollow-eyed misery that she telephoned our mother who, unlike Ruth's and her sister's, was still in England, and we were taken away next day.

I shall never forget the feeling of deliverance when the taxi came for us; it was a perfect early December day of blue and sun; fallen leaves crackled frostily under the tyres, winter colours and cobwebs sparkled with dew. It was like being snatched up to heaven in a chariot, with the taximan as the angel.

Why, I wonder now, did I approach all these efforts at capturing our childhood as fiction? Masking ourselves under other names and under storified happenings; we did not have a brother killed by a cobra as in *The River*, nor a sadistic aunt as in "Down Under the Thames"— our aunts, though perhaps mistaken over child upbringing, were immeasurably kind—nor did I ever have eyes blue as forget-me-nots. At school we never settled down, though here the story was underplayed compared to the real experience. Why did I have to disguise? Why not tell it straight?

Perhaps it was because I did not trust our story, thinking it not interesting enough? Perhaps it was because I flinched from reliving the misery we suffered; children do suffer cruelly, in a way grown-up people cannot believe; there is no more excruciating misery than a child's homesickness. Perhaps it was simply that I had inherited from my father an ineradicable bent for story-telling. I do not know the answer to any of these writing questions, but then few writers can analyse how they tick, not even for themselves.

Down Under the Thames

🌷 🌷 🌷

The wooden Swiss clock—from which a little girl in a swing hung by a chain—struck a quarter to five. "Come along," said McCann.

Deborah and Alice reluctantly picked themselves up from the rug in front of the dolls' house. They were in the middle of a "play." In 1913 George V and his Queen, Mary, had been on the throne for three years. Deborah and Alice heard much talk about them and that afternoon the dolls' house was Buckingham Palace; the two most important dolls were George and Mary and were giving a dance; Princess Mary, a rather limp doll dressed in pink tissue paper, had fainted; not having enough sawdust she was apt to faint, and two dolls' house footmen were bearing her out. It was a gorgeous play, but when McCann said "Come," Deborah and Alice knew better than to linger.

It was not long after tea but, outside, the London November dusk had already come down and the windows, where the firelight was reflected, looked deep blue, behind the little flames. The room was warm and very comfortable; a green serge cloth was on the table; the pot plant, at this time of year a tiny tree with orange berries, was set in the centre; the dappled grey paint of the rocking-horse caught the firelight, as did the brass top of the high fender where the children's stockings and white gloves were drying. There was a smell of the toast that had been made on the long toasting-fork and another smell of warm starch from McCann's apron. It all seemed dear and comfortable to Alice, but it was time to go; McCann had already opened the door into the cold passage.

In Grandmother's house the day nursery was in the basement, next door to the kitchens, while the night nursery was on the top floor, up four long flights of stairs. Alice's short legs always ached before they got to the top and the stairs were frightening; they had sombre corners where shadows lurked. Grandfather's old sword hung on the wall of the first flight and his guns were kept in a glass-fronted cupboard on the landing. Grandfather was dead and the things he had left behind personified terrifying death to Alice: the sword that, according to Deborah, had cut off people's heads and arms and legs; the guns that went "bang"—Alice was nervous even of the bangs of crackers; the fish Grandfather had caught, now stuffed, in a glass case; another case of grinning teeth, "gorilla's teeth," said McCann; worst of all, a bear that he had shot had its skin spread on the staircase wall with a great stuffed head coming out on a board. Sometimes Alice dreamed of that bear.

On the second landing she and Deborah and McCann stopped at the bathroom to save McCann carrying hot water up the two flights to the nursery. McCann washed their faces and hands, scrubbing with a face flannel, and then she ordered, "Next door."

"Go in with Alice," Deborah pleaded with McCann. "She's frightened of the seat. In India she had a little wicker chair . . ."

"She mustn't be a baby," said McCann. "Alice, go in."

This was before the days of small furniture for children, and Alice, who was only five, found life a difficult and sometimes frightening tussle with things too large and heavy for her. The lavatory had an immense mahogany seat that stretched from wall to wall, and a pan of willow-pattern china so wide and so frighteningly deep that it was enough to drown a small Alice in; worse, there was a brass handle in the seat that pulled up and released a terrifying cascade of water, enough to wash her away. "Where would I go?" she asked fearfully.

"Down drains and long, long tunnels into a big black pool, down under the Thames," said Deborah.

"*Under* the Thames?" faltered Alice. She had seen the Thames and it seemed to her an immense dark river. Now she was always terrified that by accident she would pull up the handle before she was off the seat; she would sit, in a desperate hurry, clutching her frilled drawers, her little pink bottom held as high as possible, her knees and fingers desperately clinging.

In the night nursery McCann would not light the gas for the few minutes they were there and they changed in a twilight that made them silent and depressed. The beds seemed to swim in the dusk like white birds, and the mirror, as McCann swung open the cupboard door, gave off chill white reflections. Off came their pinafores, their comfortable warm jerseys and skirts, and on went velvet frocks, brown for Deborah, blue for Alice, with heavy pleats and lace collars. McCann quickly peeled off their woollen stockings and their legs grew cold and white as they waited for the cream spun-silk ones to be put on; the silk always rasped McCann's fingers and set their teeth on edge. The stockings were fastened to the suspenders of their liberty bodices; Alice's suspenders were about two inches long and her stockings looked like Tom Thumb's. She flinched as McCann's fingers jerked the suspender buttons into their clips. McCann was always impatient with clothes; the children had a row of bruises like little blue peas up their calves from the way she jerked the buttonhook into their legs when she did up the blue kid gaiters they wore for their walks; now she snapped the elastics of their bronze dancing slippers in a crisscross round their ankles and Alice flinched again.

Poor Alice was always flinching; when her face was washed, when her frocks were buttoned and McCann's stiff starched cuffs rasped her neck, when her hair was brushed round the ringlet stick. The ringlet stick was an instrument of torture to both little girls; the hair was banded round it so tightly that it pulled the roots, then brushed, pulling tighter; when the stick was withdrawn a fine firm ringlet might be left, but the children had reddened patches on their scalps.

It was not that McCann meant to be unkind; she was, by the standards of the time, a first-rate nurse, conscientious and genuinely interested in her charges, but she had a quick temper and far too much to do. Most nurses then had a nursery-maid; McCann had none. The nurseries, separated by those flights of stairs, had to be kept to her Scottish standard of cleanliness, which was spotless. There was all the hot water to carry up, much fine sewing, and endless elaborate clothes to be washed and what McCann called "got up"; in summer, even in London, the children wore white muslin embroidered hats and dresses, starched white piqué coats; there were petticoats and drawers with lace frills to be starched, white pinafores to be threaded with ribbon. Added to this, Deborah and Alice were never left alone; even when they played in the garden McCann was required to be there. This hour, from five to six, that they spent in the drawing-room was McCann's one free time of the day and she saw that they were never late. "It's a minute to five," said McCann. "Down you go," and down they went, Alice clutching Deborah.

In the hall they passed umbrellas, a feather boa like a big caterpillar, and a row of hats, gentlemen's hats, laid on the table. "They won't *all* kiss us," said Deborah reassuringly to Alice. She knocked on the drawing-room door, opened it, and they passed through it into another world.

The sudden transition always made Alice giddy and breathless. It was some minutes before the room settled and she could take it in. It was strange that she could not get used to it, because it was always the same.

The light was always glassy and bright, either from the long windows or from the chandelier. The room was always a little hot and to Alice alarmingly full: there was always Grandmother and usually the three aunts: there were almost always ladies and gentlemen: many of the gentlemen were clergymen —the aunts were faithful church workers and even Alice was very familiar with St. Botolphs round the corner. Once, in the drawing-room, there had been a man who fascinated her; she had not known till then that grown-up people wore buttoned gaiters; she longed to ask him if he had buttonhook bruises but, "Dear Bishop, these are my two little grand-daughters," said Grandmother, and he had said, "Hah!" and given them two fingers to shake.

No matter who was there, Grandmother's opening was always the same. "Oh, children! There you are. Come and say 'How do you do.'" Amid murmurs and smiles, Deborah and

Alice would go round, giving hands and submitting to kisses. Their other hands, pinching their frocks, showed how much they minded. "I don't like the men's whiskers," said Alice privately to Deborah. "The whiskers round their mouths."

"Moustaches," said Deborah, but Alice called them "whiskers."

They knew they would be asked questions to which they must answer nicely, but when they were asked, "Have you been good girls?" Deborah would shake her curls becomingly and be silent. Alice boldly answered "Yes," which was the truth, until Aunt Gwenda said, "Oh Alice! You are conceited!"

The drawing-room was very big and to Alice very beautiful. There were long red silk curtains, chairs covered in red with black-and-gold legs, and a carpet patterned with flowers bigger than Alice's head. The fireplace was white carved marble. The wallpaper was gold-and-white striped, but it was hidden by pictures. Alice had never had time to examine them nor the cabinet that stood along one wall; in it were things with which she would dearly have liked to play, tiny cups and saucers, ivory fans, a collection of little ebony elephants, and two china shepherdesses with china rose-buds and china lace skirts. "How do they make china holes?" asked Alice. In the window was a stand of flowers and all over the room were many small tables covered with things that Alice was not allowed to touch; there were also the aunts' embroidery frames, bigger than the tables and heaped with silks, and there was a bead-embroidered bellpull that connected mysteriously with the kitchen downstairs. Once Grandmother had rung it to have Alice taken away; that was because through sheer fright she had had hiccoughs; McCann, fetched up from the kitchen, had been very cross.

Beside the piano was a little chair and a footstool; it was on these, when they had made the rounds, that the children always sat. Alice would have been content to sit there, leaning against the piano leg, her hot cheek against its fat curled mahogany as she looked at the fire, the fleecy hearth-rug, Grandmother's black skirts, at all the boots and shoes, elegantly crossed or set side by side, big boots and shoes because they hid big feet below trousers, or wide sweeping hems; she liked to look at the flowers, the ferns and potted hyacinths, azaleas or carnations, at the elephants in the cabinet and the rosy shepherdesses by them, but to sit idle and lazy was not allowed. "Sit up," said Grandmother. "The base of your back should be against the base of the chair"—Grandmother would never have said "bottom." Alice's stool had no back, but she sat upright against the piano leg. "Alice, don't twist your feet," said Aunt Gwenda.

On the rare days that the children found her quite alone Grandmother would play Spillikins with them, a game in which tiny, curved, splinter-thin pieces of wood had to be lifted with a little ivory hook from a pile without shaking it; or she would read them an enchanting tale called "The Scaramouches" about really naughty children who ran away. "Ran away?" asked Alice longingly. "Yes," said Grandmother, her eyes sparkling. Sometimes Alice thought Grandmother was not the old lady she seemed, but another little girl; but not when the aunts were there. When the aunts were there, no matter how many visitors were present, Aunt Gwenda would say, "Mother. Reading," and Grandmother would find her spectacles and beckon, first, to Deborah.

Deborah did not mind. Deborah, for her age, was an exceedingly smart little girl and with her heels together, her back held straight, her hands holding the paper up in front of her, she would read a passage from the *Times* to Grandmother with hardly a stumble, while the visitors made little noises of admiration. Then it was Alice's turn. The *Times* was too hard for Alice, but at the age when children now are being read to from *Peter Rabbit* and *Little Black Sambo,* Alice stood up and read aloud to Grandmother selected extracts from *Dombey and Son.* Alice had no idea that she was quite forward for her age; she only knew that she floundered and stumbled, grew red, forgot to keep her feet together but twisted one round the other while Grandmother tut-tutted and Aunt Gwenda looked up from her work and said, "Really! Really, Alice!"

After the children had read, Grandmother read from an instructive book such as the one about nature called *Madam How and Lady Why.* Grandmother's reading was well known and often the visitors stayed; this added to Alice's humiliation. No child was allowed to sit idle while the reading went on; they did embroidery, and when Deborah was sent to the drawer in the sofa table to get their work, Alice's heart used to sink; she never heard one word of *Madam How and Lady Why.*

The aunts were famous for their embroidery; the whole house was filled with embroidered chair covers, fire screens, tapestry cushions, table runners, but though Aunts Naomi and Gracia were clever, Gwenda, quick, dark, vivid Aunt Gwenda, was by far the best. Aunt Gwenda was making an altar cloth for the High Altar at St. Botolphs; it was worked in crimson and gold thread and its shimmering length, yards long, was kept folded up in a sheet on the floor by Aunt Gwenda's frame. It was she who taught embroidery to the children, unfortunately for Alice.

Aunt Gwenda liked Deborah; Deborah's brown eyes, crown of glossy ringlets and small, serious, pale face pleased her, but there was something about Alice's chubby littleness that enraged her. It was the same something that made the other aunts want to pick Alice up and cuddle her; Alice, pink, very plump and small, with alarmed blue eyes and brown ringlets, was appealing, but Aunt Gwenda did not think so. "She's far too babyish. She shouldn't be petted," said Aunt Gwenda, and as she was the most forceful of the aunts, Alice went unpetted. Even when, in an access of longing, she climbed on Aunt Naomi's lap and put her arms round her neck, Aunt Naomi, with Aunt Gwenda's eyes on her, put Alice down.

Alice felt the dislike and it alarmed her inexpressibly; in those days children were not articulate and Alice, still almost a baby, had no way of speaking; she only tried to avoid Aunt Gwenda, but at embroidery time she could not.

"When I was five," said Aunt Gwenda, "I embroidered this sampler," and she showed Alice a sampler, full of exquisitely stitched alphabet letters and cross-stitched roses. Deborah was deft; she was working a handkerchief sachet with violets, to be sent when finished to Father-and-Mother-in-India, but Alice was making only a traycloth, plain chain-stitch and cross-stitch in pink and blue; it showed a picture of a boy feeding two cocks and a hen. Simple as it was, it did not seem likely that it would ever get to Father-and-Mother-in-India; it was as much blood spots as stitches, knot holes and curious stains that were made by Alice's hot fingers. "Poor work!" Aunt Gwenda would say, "Poor, unfortunate work!" When the cloth in its frame had to be offered for inspection, Alice's cheeks would shake and Deborah and Grandmother knew that she was in danger of crying, but one must not cry in the drawing-room. "It's coming quite nicely," Grandmother would say quickly. "Make your stitches like pearls, like little grains of rice."

"Yes, Grandmother," and Alice somehow managed to hold out until the clock on the mantel struck six, which meant that the Swiss clock in the nursery was striking six too and Mc-Cann would come and fetch them.

Then they put their work away, chose a sweet—Grandmother called them bonbons—from a box on her table, made the rounds again pressing kisses on cheeks and whiskers, and were allowed to go blessedly upstairs to bed.

It was on the evening of this particular November dusk that Alice at last put the last stitch, a plain overstitch—"They *should* be French dots but of course *Alice* couldn't make them," said Aunt Gwenda—in the last grain of corn that the boy was feeding to the cocks and hen. She stitched it over, made it firm, giving herself a dreadful last prick, and took it to Grandmother to have the thread cut off. "Why, Alice!" said Grandmother. "It's finished!"

"Finished?" said Aunt Gracia. "Oh, Alice, at last!"

"Mother *will* be pleased," said Aunt Naomi.

"And it's beautiful," said Deborah loyally.

Alice stood, proud and flushed, while Grandmother took the traycloth out of its frame and tried to smooth the creases it had held for so long; it was soiled, bloodstained, crumpled, pricked, but it was done. Alice gave a big sigh. Then, "Let me see," said Aunt Gwenda.

Alice did not move.

"Let me see," said Aunt Gwenda more peremptorily and Alice went slowly across to her and held out the traycloth. Aunt Gwenda took it, spread it flat on her knee, and gazed at it for a long time while Alice stood beside her.

"Look at that stitch," said Aunt Gwenda jabbing her needle at it.

Alice looked.

"And that," said Aunt Gwenda. Alice flinched. "And that, and that, and that," said Aunt Gwenda and, each time, the needle jabbed and Alice flinched. "Look at the crookedness of that line: look at the little boy's nose. It isn't a nose!" said Aunt Gwenda. "It looks like a blob." She said "blob" with such venom that Alice jumped and looked hard at the little boy's nose. "Disgraceful—careless—dirty—work," said Aunt Gwenda. She turned to her frame and picked up her embroidery scissors that were shaped like a bird, its long beak the blades. "Alice, do you know what I am going to do?" asked Aunt Gwenda.

Alice made a little noise that might have been "Yes." She watched while the scissors went swiftly along the work, the sharp beak snipping out the stitches. Aunt Gwenda's quick, clever fingers picked out the pink and blue threads and dropped them as if they were dirty, into the basket that stood by her frame.

"Gwenda!" said Grandmother, protesting, and a visitor said, "Oh, poor lamb!"

"She must learn," said Aunt Gwenda, with a heightened colour, and when the last thread was out, she shook out the cloth. "There, Alice," she said, "you can put it back in the frame and start it all over again. *That* will teach you!"—and Aunt Gwenda picked up her needle, turned to her altar cloth, and began to work. Her needle made a firm plucking noise in the silent room.

"We will put it back in the frame tomorrow," said Grandmother in a trembling voice to Alice.

Alice, with the crumpled little cloth in her hand, did not answer. Her cheeks were shaking; suddenly she went scarlet and her eyes, thought Deborah, looked like forget-me-nots grown miraculously angry.

"Come and sit down, Alice," said Aunt Gracia kindly, but Alice went to the door.

"Where are you going?" asked Aunt Gwenda.

"Upstairs," said Alice in a choked voice, turning the knob.

"Heavens! Children!" said Aunt Gwenda, and impatiently to Grandmother, "Ring for McCann."

"I can go by myself," said Alice and went.

"She's going to cry," said Deborah. "Past the bear and the guns! By herself! Oh, let me go," she cried, jumping up and falling over Alice's stool in her haste, but, "Sit down, Deborah," said Aunt Gwenda sharply. "If she must be such a baby, leave her alone. Well, Mother, why not read?" she asked.

It seemed a long time, a long reading of *Madam How and Lady Why*, till Alice came back, but at last she came. She shut the door behind her, using both hands on the knob, and went to her stool. Her eyes still looked like those angry forget-me-nots and she was breathing hard, but she was quiet. She sat down and fixed her eyes on Grandmother to listen, but Aunt Gwenda was staring at her.

"Where is your traycloth?" asked Aunt Gwenda.

Alice took her eyes off Grandmother; she looked down at the floor where her feet were twisted as usual, crossed her hands over her stomach as if she squeezed a secret to herself, and did not reply.

"Where is it?" asked Aunt Gwenda.

Alice's eyelids were like two pink seals over her eyes as she looked at the floor.

"Where is your traycloth? Answer!" commanded Aunt Gwenda.

Alice lifted her eyes and looked at Aunt Gwenda. "Down under the Thames," said Alice.

❧

The Little Fishes

❦   ❦   ❦

When our mother had driven away, we were sent with a lay sister up to the nun in charge of the dormitories, Sister Irene. Sister Irene had a very white skin, and the banded coif she wore showed the hollows in her cheeks and made her grey eyes look big; we had never seen anyone as tall, as graceful, or as cool. "These are the two little Goddens," said the lay sister.

Sister Irene looked down at us. "What queer little fishes!" she said.

There is a tinted photograph taken of us just before we went to school; the photographer knocked our heads gently together—in those days that was the way sisters were posed—and we have come out as two sallow, thin, small girls, cheek to cheek, with too much hair and wide-open eyes. Ruth's eyes were like the spaniel's in the poem, "eyes like mottoes," eloquent and sincere; they impelled you to live up to them, but in the photograph our eyes have an appalled look; perhaps it was with the swiftness of what had happened to us; a month ago we had been part of the small contented world of the Indian town we lived in; perhaps it was an unreal world, but to us it had been halcyon. We had been the most important Europeans there and our father ruled imperially; our mother was queen and we, quite naturally, were princesses. "What shall I call the king when I get to England?" I had asked Mother before we sailed, "Shall I call him 'Your Majesty' or just plain 'George'?"

It was a shock when we reached England to find we did not know the king, that we were an ordinary middle-class family, not special or interesting in any way. Then Ruth and I were torn from Father and Mother, who seemed to take it as a matter of course, and we were sent to school at the Anglican Convent of St. Monica's. It was the end of our childhood. In the photograph our mouths are slightly open, which gives us the look of two little fishes gasping. "What odd little fishes, out of the water," said Sister Irene.

We must have looked odd. The school coats were thicker than anything we had ever worn and we moved stiffly in them like marionettes; their dark blue made us look even more sallow than we were. We had not worn gloves before and we held our fingers straight out in our new brown kid gloves. "Curl your fingers round," said Sister Irene. "Unbend them." Our noses and eyes were swollen and pink with weeping and cold, and our pie-dish hats would not sit down on our curly hair. "That hair must be tied back!" said Sister Irene, and before she took us downstairs, she plaited it for us; it was to be one of our disgraces that we did not know how to plait. My hair soon adapted itself but Ruth's obstinately curled in its plait; it was a real pigtail. Ruth was older, less adaptable; it was altogether harder for Ruth than for me.

"Why do we have to go to school?" we had asked desperately. "Why in England, not India?"

We knew the answer to that. It was the Climate and the Accent.

Ruth was thirteen and I was twelve, but from the torrid heat, we were undersized, thin and sickly. We spoke, it seemed, in a clipped singsong way that they called "chi-chi"; Sister Margaret, our form mistress, said it was atrocious.

"In the merry month of May," said Sister Margaret, in smooth bell-like tones.

"In-th-merree-munt-ov-Maiee," we said after her.

"No! No! No!" cried Sister Margaret, and the whole form shouted with laughter; soon, whenever we spoke, we were corrected by everyone.

"If you live in a chi-chi place no one knows you are chi-chi," said Ruth longingly.

Every day India seemed more far away, more beautiful and dear: that little town instead of this ugly English one: our dear house with the high rooms and stone floors and heavy shutters instead of this labyrinthine building with its red brick towers and cross. We thought of our Indian garden with the swing under the mango tree; we saw the tangles of flowers, morning glory and quisqualis and jasmine and hibiscus and bamboo, instead of these bare games-fields, the asphalt playground and gravelled walks. In India we had had animals: Sadie the mongoose, and the ponies; we had servants, our fat, useless, kind nurse, Moti Ayah, and Ram Prasad, the gateman, who was our best friend; here there was no one for us to pet, no one to pet us.

St. Monica's was big, up-to-date, and prosaic; it seemed unutterably chill and stark to us. There were classrooms with long windows and deal furniture; a gymnasium where we spent our recreation; a refectory that had a red tiled floor, whitewashed walls, and a macabre picture of the "Last Supper." There was a library where only the big girls were allowed, a cloakroom of lockers, hooks, and basins and a drove of lavatories where the doors did not quite come down to the floor; if you lingered in one—perhaps to shed a few tears—a girl was sure to look underneath. The dormitories upstairs were divided into cubicles by iron rails hung with ghostly white curtains that were allowed to be drawn only when we washed. There was no privacy anywhere; a lay sister even sat in the bathroom while we had our twice weekly bath.

There were long corridors with pale-green distempered walls and marble statues of the saints; as the winter went on, these saints looked colder and colder. One of the rules was that we had to be silent in the corridors, and if a nun came by, we had to stand quite still until she had passed. There were many of these niceties of behaviour, all difficult to remember, and Ruth and I committed countless solecisms. We did not know, for instance, whether we were Oxford or Cambridge, Liberal or Conservative, or even whether we liked Winnie, the head girl, more than Cynthia, the games captain. "I don't like either," said Ruth. She said it aloud, which was heresy. The whole school was divided into factions over Winnie and Cynthia; there were queues to kiss them goodnight. I should rather have liked to kiss Winnie but I did not dare. "Winnie has pimples," said Ruth. She did not say how she felt about Cynthia, and as far as we were concerned, they stayed unkissed.

The house was peopled by black-and-white-dressed nuns or blue-dressed girls, big and little; we were cut off from the outside world and when anyone came from it, a mother or a workman in their worldly clothes, they looked quite odd. The day was measured and tolled out by the bell which Sister Irene rang up and down the corridors; at seven each morning, before it finished ringing, we had to be out of bed, standing on our cubicle mats with our beds stripped. That sudden impact with the morning, the cold and dark and noise, was like a nightmare to me and Ruth; it stunned us for the rest of the day. Having, as we felt, exposed ourselves, standing shivering by our beds, we were allowed to collect water in our basins, pull our curtains, and go into our cubicles to wash and dress. Ruth and I were always late because our fingers were stiff with cold, we were not used to so many clothes, and when the ten minutes were up and we paraded outside our dormitories, we were always buttoned wrongly and our hair was not done. "I suppose you had an Ayah to help you dress," said Sister Irene as she twisted us round and her quick fingers plaited, while the juniors, little girls of nine and ten, giggled. "We had an Ayah," said Ruth," but she didn't help us dress, she didn't have to. In India people are not in a hurry," said Ruth. "There is time to dress and it is warm."

Warm! Under Sister Irene's hands I shut my eyes; I felt sun, warm in the puffs of wind that brought a hot sweet scent of the flowers like yellow fuzz-balls that grew on the thorn trees in our garden. I smelled sun on grass and leaves, I felt warm dust under my bare feet and the feeling of house-stones hot with sun. "Look, she's crying!" said the gay little juniors, and I had an order mark.

In one week we collected more order marks than other girls in a term; we had order marks for answering back, for unpunctuality, for being untidy, and finally we were sent in to the Sister Superior, Sister Gertrude. "You must learn that there is a place and time for everything and a way of doing everything," said Sister Gertrude severely.

I have seen many headmistresses since then, some of them awe-inspiring, but I have never seen one as awful, in the old sense of the word, as Sister Gertrude. It is strange to think of a nun as arrogant and unkind, but she was both. I suppose she was chosen as a disciplinarian and the Order thought her good at heart; she was not good at heart and even to look at her made one afraid. She was a big choleric woman with a red face and curiously soft and puffy cheeks that, when she was angry, seemed to swell—and she was often angry. Fortunately she was usually remote, like God; she took prayers, and at the midday meal, she sat at the centre of the high table in a chair with a high back like a throne. For the rest, she stayed in her study and at four o'clock one of the prefects carried her a tray of tea; for us, Sister Gertrude's might could be measured by the fact that these dazzling great girls had to wait on her. When she made announcements at prayers Winnie stood at her right side, handing her papers, and Cynthia stood on the left with the games lists. If I ever pictured God in those days with the Archangels Gabriel and Michael, I am sure I saw them as Cynthia and Winnie attending Sister Gertrude.

From the very first there was trouble between Sister Gertrude and Ruth—"a time and a place for everything," said the Sister.

Ruth looked at her with sincere and thoughtful eyes. "But it takes time to learn the places," said Ruth gently.

Ruth had more order marks than I, chiefly because she was more loyal to our upbringing, more honest. I found ways of avoiding trouble and I tried to help her but this was something that was not allowed; the slow, the weak, the timid had to be left as victims to themselves. St. Monica's was a convent school founded on religion; twice a day we went to chapel, three times a day the Angelus sounded through the school and we had prayers in the big gymnasium every day. Sister Gertrude read the lessons and the girls took it in turn to read the collect for the day—not, of course, either of us because of the chi-chi accent. "Blessed are the meek," read Sister Gertrude, or "God has chosen the foolish things of the world to confound the wise," "God hath chosen the weak . . . things which are despised hath God chosen." A little feeble-minded girl, Florence, was very much despised; Sister Gertrude treated her with heart-rending coldness. "The first shall be last," read Sister Gertrude, but the work and life of the school, its conduct and lessons and games, seemed founded on a precept that was quite opposite; there was a scrabble to be first, to be best, to be successful, and it was shameful to be last, to be slow, to be weak, to be little. "What, Ruth, last *again!*" Sister Margaret would say and, "Do you want to be put down to a junior?" It was like the game of musical chairs we played on Feast days; when the music stopped you had at all cost to get yourself a chair. Ruth and I were quite hopeless at it, especially Ruth; she would stand politely and let anyone take her chair, even a junior. "But she is little," Ruth would say when they told her angrily not to be a fool.

By degrees we learned that there was something that reconciled these extremes: it was called "being sporting." "You and your sister really must learn to be sports," said the mighty Cynthia to me. Probably no two children who ever went to school were less sports than we; to begin with we were shocking cowards. My first day on the hockey field a ball hit me on the chin and I cried; after that I would not play. It did not seem to me sense.

"The ball's too hard," I said.

"You mustn't say that," said Cynthia appalled.

"But it *is* too hard," I said.

"It's hard but you mustn't say it," said Cynthia. "You must be sports."

It was hopeless; we were not sports but we were sneaks; when Sister Margaret asked about an overturned inkpot or a scribble on the blackboard "Who did this?" Ruth and I answered obligingly, "Greta Robinson" or "Mary Smith." How were we to know that Greta or Mary would be made to stand on the rostrum in the gymnasium in front of everybody or be sent to bed with the juniors or have dry bread for tea? When, in India, my father had asked, "Who did this?" and we had said "Ruth," or "Harriet," nothing had ever happened. The Indian way of bringing up children might be summed up as "Love them and leave them alone." Perhaps through living in India our parents had adopted a little of that way; at St. Monica's nobody loved us and nobody left us alone.

We were not even allowed to walk alone, and strangely, not with a sister. The school went out two by two in a crocodile, and as no one else ever chose Ruth or me, we would wait, hanging about with the other rejects, until a nun paired us off; Ruth was either made to walk with the nun or else a Chinese girl, Ansie, with whom nobody wanted to walk because she spoke very little English and was even more sullen and silent than we. I usually had Florence, who never spoke at all. I grew quite fond of Florence; I could tell her stories and as she was silent, the stories were not interrupted; it was like writing aloud.

The girls in front or the girls behind must have listened to my stories as we moved along in our blue-coated, blue-hatted crocodile, for soon I was being asked to tell them in recreation, in the garden breaks, in sewing hour, especially stories about India. It was so intoxicating to be suddenly interesting that it went to my head. I told everything that the girls wanted to hear about India: about rajahs, elephants, howdahs, faithful brown servants, curries, tigers, and snakes.

It led to trouble: ". . . with his foot on the python, my father looked up," I was saying one day. "He looked up and saw, not one, but three tigers."

"That's not true," said a girl with some sense.

"I swear it's true . . ." but there was Sister Irene and she beckoned me.

"Come with me," said Sister Irene. Feeling very small and chilled, I went.

The nuns used public opinion as a rod and I was publicly shamed. As a branded liar I was told to wear my class badge upside down.

"All people are liars," said Ruth and wore hers upside down too. When told she must not, she still did it and she was sent to Sister Gertrude.

"This spirit must be broken," Sister Gertrude told her, and proud, mature Ruth was sent to bed with the juniors, and as an extra punishment, we were not allowed to take part in the school operetta, "H.M.S. Pinafore," though, even if we had not been punished, we should not have been allowed to sing in it, because of our chi-chi accents. Now we spent rehearsal time isolated in a classroom with Florence and Ansie, in charge of a lay sister called Boots. I thought it was her real name and called her that until Sister Irene heard me, but Boots never minded being called "Boots"; almost like Moti Ayah she never minded what we said or did. Those were the most peaceful times of the week; the sounds of "Little Buttercup" and "His sisters and his cousins and his aunts" came only dimly to our ears; Boots let us sit warm and quiet and peaceful near the fire;

we could read or make Christmas cards; she let me read my poems to her and said that they were lovely.

That term was only eleven weeks long but if it had been eleven years we could not have learned more in sadness and duplicity. It was the autumn term and as our characters, already black, grew steadily blacker, the English weather grew more colourless, colder, and more wintry. At first there had been October days when, with the leaves turning and the air blue and clear with thin sun, England had seemed, though cold, beautiful to us, but November was grey; the rain beat down in long hard needles or else there was fog and damp, and so we passed into December.

Perhaps some of our misery was physical: Ruth had a cough; we were stupid with head colds and we had chilblains; we looked at our swollen purple hands with horror. I learned the piano with Sister Loyala and when she made me stretch my hands, the chilblains cracked and bled. Sister Irene tried her best to make us hardy; she gave us malt and cod-liver oil but the taste stayed in our throats and it was as difficult to get down as was the food; from the beginning we had disliked and dreaded the school food. "What *is* it?" we asked the first time we saw one of the school puddings, suet encasing rhubarb or suet with raisins; we were not being captious, we really wanted to know and though we did not believe the answers, "dead baby" and "spotted dog," they made it harder to eat the puddings. Nothing was allowed to be left on our plates and we choked with dead baby and spotted dog.

Perhaps it was the cold too that made us stupid. St. Monica's was noted for its thorough teaching and good examination results and in the framework of our class syllabus we toiled most of the day. Ruth and I were in the bottom class of the

senior school; they could not have put us in lower without
making us juniors and we were palpably too old and big for
that. If I were backward, Ruth was more backward still. I
burned with pity for Ruth; the mark results and class positions
were read out at prayers every Monday morning with horrible
publicity, and the bottom of our class was always the same:
Florence bottom with Ansie, then Ruth, then me. "And Florence is mentally deficient," said Sister Margaret, "and Ansie
cannot speak English!" Ruth seemed to have fallen into a
paralysis. In India, working with father, she had been good at
lessons; now, listening to her stumbling, frightened replies, I
could not believe that this was Ruth; England seemed to have
shocked her into a block of stupidity. I did not wonder that
Sister Margaret grew impatient. I managed better; I had a parrot quickness that Ruth, who was more honest, did not possess.
I found that the way to cope, for instance, with literature—the
Book of Ballads and *Julius Caesar*—was to learn them both by
heart. I could gabble.

> "You-all-do-know-this-mantle-I-remember-
> the-first-time-ever-Caesar-put-it-on-
> 'Twas-on-a-summer's-evening-in-his-tent-
> that-day-he-overcame-the-Nervii."

"Who are the Nervii?" asked Ruth.
"It doesn't matter," I said and began on the Ballads.

> "He-was-a-braw-gallant
> and-he-played-at-the-glove."

"What glove?" asked Ruth, "and what's 'braw'?"
I also learned, very artfully and cleverly, to cheat. I used to
look over at the papers of the girls next to me and copy. Sister

Margaret was taken in and thought I was improving. "That's the way," she said encouragingly.

"One day you will be found out," said Ruth.

It sounded all too probable but I was so miserable already I did not think it would make any difference. All the same I think I worried about it. For the first time I learned what it was like to lie awake at nights. There was a big clock in the gymnasium that chimed every quarter, like St. Joan's voices in the Bernard Shaw play:

> "You-must-go-on,
> You-shall-save-France."

I used to lie and listen to quarter after quarter, and then to the slow striking of the hour; One—another long, long waste of quarters—Two—sometimes I heard a little sound from Ruth but we dared not speak to one another. All around us girls were sleeping and breathing lustily; far away on the map and as meaningless as its paper were Father and Mother, Moti Ayah, Ram Prasad, India. Tears used to trickle down my nose and soak the pillow. "Sick for home . . ." I was only twelve but to the depths of my being I found out what those words meant.

Perhaps our greatest shock was that Father and Mother seemed to take it for granted that we should be unhappy. "School is always like that at first," wrote Mother. "You will get used to it, then you will like it," wrote Father. "Like it!" said Ruth as if she had been stung and she said, "I shall never forgive them for this. Never!" It was the first time we had known that a father and mother could be against their children; indeed, with great love and tenderness, they made things worse.

They had decided that perhaps it was the religious life of the Convent that was a little too strict. The religion was one of the few things we really understood; though there had been no Christian church near us in India, we had seen plenty of religion and it seemed to us entirely natural. In the general austerity and chill of St. Monica's, the colour and warmth of the chapel were beautiful; there were stained glass and lace, deep crimson carpets, lit candles and music. The nuns and choir sang, we thought, like angels and the religion was romantic; for chapel we wore little round caps of blue, like medieval pages, and on Sundays, black net veils that made us feel like madonnas or nuns. Feast days were especially glorious, with lessons interrupted and processions and chapel at odd times. Then Mother wrote to Sister Gertrude asking for us to be excused from chapel.

For the nuns this was the last straw; offended and shocked they shut us out. Now we were really outcast; even the juniors went to chapel, even Florence and Ansie. Ansie, missionary trained, was devout; she had a Chinese bible that she read from the back to the front. We were horribly and conspicuously alone. Sister Gertrude's announcements would be, "Tomorrow is the Feast of the Presentation of the Blessed Virgin Mary. The whole school will attend Mass at eleven . . . except the Goddens," or "There will be Vespers after tea tonight for everyone except the juniors . . . the juniors and the *Goddens*." If she had said "the barbarians" she could not have sounded more scornful and we burned in our heathen shame.

Willy-nilly we spent more and more time with Boots. With the foreigner and the deficient we were beginning to sink under the weight of degradation when Ruth had her famous battle with Sister Gertrude.

One afternoon there was a rehearsal for "H.M.S. Pina-fore"; the five of us outcasts were happily at work in the peaceful classroom when the door opened and in swept Sister Gertrude.

Like rabbits on springs, Boots, Ansie, Ruth and I shot to our feet and stood; Florence gave her silly slow smile but sat still.

"Stand up," snapped Sister Gertrude at her. Florence looked bewildered and Boots pulled her up.

Sister Gertrude had a visitor with her, an old priest who seemed very small and frail beside the big Sister. He was dressed in a black cassock and biretta and wore pince-nez and black woollen gloves; when he spoke his voice sounded as if it rustled. He smiled at us and said faintly, "So these are some of the dear girls?"

Sister Gertrude's glance swept over us—nothing of Sister Gertrude's ever moved, it swept—her eyes swept over humble Boots, glowering Chinese Ansie, over Florence, Ruth, and me. Perhaps Florence with her smile, her chin that was always a little wet with saliva, her round blue eyes and stringy hair, exasperated her. "These," she said cuttingly, "are the scum of the school."

Boots looked at the floor, Ansie did not understand, Florence smiled; I went scarlet as I always did, but Ruth put up her hand. She held it up unwaveringly. Sister Gertrude did not take any notice but the old priest stopped. He looked at Sister and then at Ruth. There was a pause. Her chin high, Ruth continued to hold up her hand. At last, "Well?" asked Sister Gertrude.

"Please, Sister," said Ruth, breathing very quickly. "We are not scum."

There was silence. Sister Gertrude's cheeks had swelled; I

could see white patches round Ruth's nostrils and she quivered; though my own cheeks were hot, I was cold with fear. I think Sister Gertrude would have gone out, but the priest stood between her and the door. He stood there looking at her. He looked steadily, without speaking. The silence went on and presently Sister Gertrude, in a voice like any schoolgirl, said to Ruth, "I beg your pardon. I shouldn't have said that. No one is scum."

"Thank you, my daughter," said the priest and they went out.

A year later another photograph was taken of us to send to Mother and Father. It was taken out of doors; in it we were wearing our school coats and gloves, but as if they fitted us easily; our hats sat neatly on our pigtailed heads, though Ruth's pigtail still curled; we had plaited our hair ourselves. At that time Ruth was Oxford, I was Cambridge; we were both Liberals. I liked Winnie while Ruth, if she had ever admitted it, would most certainly have chosen Cynthia. We had grown taller and fatter, perhaps from Sister Irene's malt, and our mouths were firmly shut. We were two little fishes, breathing naturally through our gills and swimming in the sea.

❦

Why Not Live Sweetly?

❧ and ❧

Telling the Time by the Starlings

Perhaps all English writers born in the provinces have
wanted, when they were young, to "come up to London
—for me it was an even farther away dream than for
most because my girlhood and young womanhood
were spent in India, chiefly in the remote Bengali town
in which my father lived and worked. When we did come
"home," as England was called, though it was never really
"home" to us, it was for "leaves," spent, as my father was a
dedicated fisherman and hunter, in North Wales, or in
the Hebrides, with visits to the Sussex where I was born.

I often think of myself, that young girl in India, a
complete misfit in the riding, swimming, tennis- and
golf-playing club world around her, eating out her heart
for Bloomsbury and living on those never-to-be-glimpsed
great names of the twenties and thirties; Virginia and
Leonard Woolf, E.M.Forster, the Sitwells—I carried
Façade about with me. When I came to London at last,
it was too late. Years of living almost in solitude—on a
lonely Himalayan tea-garden, out in the country in
Kashmir, and on those Cornish moors—had made me
farouche, shy almost to ungraciousness, and perhaps a bit
wild, thoroughly unsociable. I could not talk to people,

63

nor they to me. Everything I did was wrong; in fact I
made all the mistakes most writers make at eighteen or in
their early twenties; what is normal at that age, though,
can become disastrous when one is getting on for forty
with two children to bring up, and I went through a bad,
if salutary, time.

These two short stories were, I think, a reaction
against trying to live and keep up with that city
environment (which I have since come to love). "Why
Not Live Sweetly?" was the result of a short experience
of living in one of London's vast blocks of flats—"a
human filing cabinet." "Telling the Time by the
Starlings" was homesickness for the remote life of the
moors and Welsh mountains—but I knew a little dark
Welsh girl like Gwyneth.

Why Not Live Sweetly?

🌷 🌷 🌷

If anything could have been more surprising to her than her marriage to Eddie, it was living here, in town, with him. She could not account for it at all; sometimes she stopped in the city streets looking and wondering how she had come there, and every morning, when she woke, she thought she was still at home.

"Not at home," said jealous Eddie. "That was your old home. This is your home now."

She said slowly, "I always meant to marry Roger."

"I caught you, right under his nose," said Eddie, gleefully. "Poor old slow-coach Roger."

"Yes, he was slow," she said that slowly too.

She had lived in the country all her life, yet she was not most people's idea of a country girl; but then most people did not know her inland West country, its silences and depths, the wildness of its greys and blues and browns, soft colours, but wild, its strong life. To those who did not know it, she was a country girl. "And she won't translate," they said. "People from there don't." But Eddie had caught her in his quick way, and brought her, without a thought, to town.

Eddie was a journalist, and if there were anything she could have regretted about Eddie, it was that; his dexterous use of words made him foreign to her; gradually she came to have a strong feeling about words, a feeling that they left nothing to be itself, but coloured, twisted, changed, distorted everything. "But they shouldn't do that," she said. "Words have meanings."

As she began to realize the, to her, extraordinary strangeness of her new life, she felt it enclosing her; she did not remember being enclosed by life before. At times she was filled with panic and she was troubled by this sense of words. Eddie knew endless words and she did not; Eddie wrote six hundred words, eight hundred, a thousand every day, undeterred that next day, or the day after, the newspaper was crumpled into a ball, or used to light the fire, or to line a shelf or wrap up parcels.

"Never mind," said Eddie. "I can always write some more; have to," he said ruefully, but he enjoyed it. He rejoiced in his wit and quickness and easy flow.

"But . . . it ought not to be quick," she said. "It should be slow and hard."

"A good thing for us it isn't!"

"But it should be. It should be slow and hard, absolutely sure and rather perilous." She was so much in earnest that her cheeks were flushed. "Like mining," she said. "Or growing apple trees, or like a birth, with the head coming slowly, slowly through the pelvis."

"Oh, my sweet!"

"It should."

"I'm not a writer," said Eddie. "I'm a word-monger. You mustn't try to turn me into what I'm not."

"No," she said. "But . . . I have to think and, yes, I have to be what I am, too."

"You are my wife," said Eddie, kissing her. "You can't get out of that."

As she went on being Eddie's wife she began fitting words to people as if people were living words, different words. Some are just "if" and "which" and "this" and "that," she thought, but some have more meaning, serious or gay, or sad, or bitter, or happy, or healing. That bristly apoplectic old man is "battle," she thought, and that woman with the quiet withdrawn face and the long hands and the grey eyes is "twilight," though it is difficult for anyone to give out his or her full meaning, especially in a city where they are jumbled together.

She told this to Eddie.

"What will you think of next?" he said.

She was able to tell him that too. Today she had thought that living in a town was prose, while living in the country was poetry.

Eddie said that was going too far. "Living in a city can be poetry too."

"Not to everyone, Eddie," she said, and suddenly, "Living in a block of flats like this is journalese."

That annoyed Eddie, but she had to go on.

"Columns and columns of people live in these flats," she said.

"Where is all this leading?" he demanded. "You are perfectly happy here."

"Yes, Eddie."

"Are you?"

"Yes. Of course I'm happy but . . ."

"But what?"

"I . . . don't quite know."

"If people are words," said the exasperated Eddie, "you are 'but,' always wanting to fly round the corner." Then he looked at her face and relented. "You mustn't think so much about home—your old home," he corrected himself. "You must think of us, of me and you."

She did not tell him that she did not have to think of home, nor of the village, nor the woods above the river in the valley that ran down from the moor, because she had never left her home, nor could she; she knew that now. It was only when Eddie described it, as he often did to their friends, that it drew far away and became a little distorted and so quite out of truth.

"It's a dimpled country," said Eddie, picturesquely.

"Oh, Eddie! It's not!" She could have cried.

"I don't know how else to describe it," said Eddie, and he went on to describe moor, woods, valley, village, river, always going farther away from truth. "Cornfields radiant and green," said Eddie, "sun striking the mica in the old grey walls."

Did the sun strike the mica in the walls? She wondered. She had never noticed it. She looked at Eddie to ask him, and then she saw he did not know.

He began to talk of the trees, the fine old unhampered trees, beeches, oaks, and ash, and in a surge a sound rose up in her to contradict him, the very truth of those trees that he could not possibly know, like the sound of the wind in their branches.

"Gentle . . ." she caught the word as Eddie said it, though perhaps he had not said it about the trees at all.

Not gentle; strong, passionately strong, she cried silently.

The strength of her feeling surprised her. Afterwards she tried not to think of it; it was, as yet, only a feeling.

It is only the feeling I get from the trees round my home, she told herself. It's natural I should feel it, being homesick, but its strength terrified her. It had as yet no expression, no meaning, no words, but she knew its words would come and when they came, though Eddie might think them gentle and yielding, she knew they would be inexorable. Yet she loved Eddie and he loved her. Even if he came into a room crowded with people, his eyes searched for her and found her; he had young eyes, brave and blue and a little hard, so determined that they were almost insolent, but they grew tender when they looked at her.

Eddie worked hard, pouring his words into the stream that came out in the print of his paper every morning:

> the talks that were resumed at eight o'clock last night were again held under the semi-secret conditions first introduced for Thursday's informal gathering. A British spokesman said late last night, "An understanding was reached that nothing should be said about the discussions beyond the fact that they will be continued tomorrow in another informal meeting."

> . . . the Russian delegate was absent . . .

> . . . an early settlement is unlikely . . .

The first words of a poem that she had learned long ago in school came into her head.

> I had a dove and the sweet dove died;
> And I have thought it died of grieving:
> O, what could it grieve for? . . .

What had that to do with it? With her and Eddie?

In the mansion flats where they lived, one could be woken every morning on the telephone; all internal calls were free; it was part of the service. They were called at seven; Eddie usually woke at once, but she took longer because she persisted in waking first in her room at home and had that preliminary struggle before she knew she was here in the flat. They found the morning papers and the milk in its neatly sealed bottles waiting for them in the service lift. After breakfast the service maid came in with the vacuum cleaner to do the rooms. They could telephone down to the shops on the ground floor for their provisions, their flowers, cigarettes, stationery, theatre tickets, and taxis. There was a valeting service, hairdressers, and a shoeshine. If they preferred not to cook, they could choose between the snack bar and the restaurant. For amusement there was dancing, swimming, tennis, and a wireless in every room.

"What more could you want?" asked Eddie.

Not more—far, far less, she would have said.

"You have to admit it's convenient," said Eddie. He said that often, and every time he said it she distrusted it still more, and disliked it.

"Convenient and expedient," she said aloud. "Those words are like traps."

"Traps?"

"Yes, traps. Once you let them catch you, you never get away again."

"Nonsense. We live here because we want to be free."

"Are you free?" she asked.

"Yes, I am," said Eddie indignantly, "and so, I hope, are you."

She did not answer. That little poem had come again like an echo into her head, and now it did not seem irrelevant, nor little either.

> . . . Its feet were tied
> With a silken thread of my own hand's weaving: . . .

But Eddie didn't weave it, she thought. Nor did I. It was woven for us—of us, she corrected herself; but it was his doing, she thought. I was meant to marry Roger. Eddie says himself he caught me.

"No one ever noticed you or saw you at home, at your old home," Eddie was fond of saying. "You were nobody there."

She did not tell him that he was wrong. She was not a nobody at home, she was herself. Maybe, she thought, slowly, I should have stayed for Roger.

"They wouldn't know you now," said Eddie. He came closer. "You pretty thing," he said.

She felt as if she were struggling, though she was quiet under his hands. "Kiss me," said Eddie, and she kissed him. "I love you," said Eddie. "You know that."

"Yes, but . . ." and she said helplessly, "It doesn't make any difference."

He drew back quickly, offended from his ears to his soul. "Then you do want to go home."

As he said that, the surge of the wind in the trees rose up in her again so that she no longer heard it, but was in it, wheeling, tumbling, gliding, rising, borne up and away, free into a distance that was still home; borne up, borne away, and at the same time she gave herself a desperate command and heard her voice, stifled and small, answer from far down below her, somewhere on earth with Eddie, "No," she heard herself answer. "No, I don't want to go home."

Eddie sat down and took her on his knee, and began to talk. Eddie knew all the words and his words now were reasonable, kind, sensible, and powerful; they had Eddie's potency and determination and quickness. She listened and all she said was, "Yes, Eddie. No, Eddie. Yes, Eddie."

"People are not all the same," said Eddie.

"No, Eddie."

"At the same time, we must be adaptable. There is no reason why we shouldn't be."

> Why, pretty thing! would you not live with me?

It came irresistibly into her mind.

"We can adapt ourselves to anything," said Eddie, and his words went on so fluently that she began to have the idea he was reading from a newspaper. She started to fidget, and Eddie, disappointed but still kind, brought what he had said to a sensible conclusion. He looked hopefully into her face, and as he looked, hope faded. "Now say 'but,'" said Eddie.

She had to say it. "But, Eddie, I am not that kind of person."

"What kind of person?"

"Adaptable."

"You must be."

"But—if I am not?"

"You must learn to be."

She was silent. She was thinking that if she were the word "but" then Eddie was "must." She sighed.

> . . . I kissed you oft and gave you white peas; . . .

"And they were useless to it, I expect, poor thing," she said.

"What did you say?" asked Eddie. "Never mind. Kiss me."

She kissed him again, but though his lips drew hers, the poem would not leave her. She thought of it as Eddie kissed her, trying to remember its last line. "All the same you are sweet," said Eddie, "Sweet."

After he had gone, she went to the bookshelves and took down his big dictionary. She looked up those two words "must" and "but."

"Must: to be obliged, forced physically or morally." Physically *and* morally, she thought.

"But: without; except; besides; only; still;" weak, wishful, small words that, in her case she admitted, flew out of the sentence without explaining themselves. Of course, "but" hasn't a chance against "must," she thought. Not a chance.

The sounds of the mammoth building came steadily through the windows, the ceiling, the floor, and the walls. Though they were dulled, partly cut off by sound-proof thickness, she could hear telephones, radios playing afternoon music, lifts, bells, a vacuum cleaner in the corridor; she shut her eyes but now, though she strained to catch it, the sound of the wind in the trees was growing fainter. It must grow faint. I must forget it, she told herself.

She opened her eyes and she saw that the afternoon sun, striking down to her window past the wall of the next block, had cast the shadow shape of the window on the floor. It was a modern window of long panels joined with steel, and its shape made a pattern of bars.

As she looked at them, clearly, over the fading sound of the trees, the last line of the poem came:

> . . . Why not live sweetly, as in the green trees?

Why not live sweetly?
Why not?
Why not?

❦

Telling the Time by the Starlings

🌷 🌷 🌷

The alarm clock went at seven, breakfast was at seven forty-five, and he caught the eight twenty-six up to town; the bank opened its doors at ten, closed them at three o'clock; he took an hour off for lunch at a quarter to one and, if things ran easily, the daily balance worked out, he caught the five-fifty train down; supper was at seven and they listened to the late news. The last thing he did at night was to wind up his watch. In spite of this attentiveness to time, he was usually tired; lately he was unusually tired.

"What's wrong with you, Charles?" asked Sophie, his wife. "Sometimes you look vague."

"Vague? Don't be silly. How could I do my job and be vague?"

"Well, don't growl at me," said Sophie, but she was right. It was true that sometimes he did feel vague. Vague thoughts filled his mind or, rather, did not fill it but made rifts in it, rifts that he could not define but that shed, as if they were light, a clarity on the life he led as if he were meant to look at it. But I'm too tired to look, thought Charles, and I have always led it, though I don't know why. That "why," too, was in his mind lately.

"You need a tonic," said Sophie.

"For what?" Charles found he had almost shouted.

"All right. All right." Sophie was startled. "I just thought it might make you more lively."

Charles grunted and buried himself in the newspaper.

Even the papers were divided into morning and evening papers: dailies, weeklies, monthlies. Soon we shall have hourlies, thought Charles, "Digests" so that we can read them in a minute. Tabloid. Everything in tabloid so that we can swallow it in seconds, without tasting. Nothing tastes, nothing! But it should. It did once, or did it? And he shut his eyes. What was that thing? ". . . and yet I know, where'er I go, that there hath pass'd away a glory from the earth." That was it. "The power and the glory," he said aloud.

"A crossword clue?" asked Sophie.

Sophie, thought Charles, had palings round her mind, and his mind began to dwell upon walls; walls were for prisons, but he thought of moat walls, old and clear and cool, holding water; he saw red brick kitchen-garden walls with plums and peaches trained against them, and granite walls on moors and mountains, built from the granite intrinsic to those moors and mountains. Palings cost little to put up and were easily tacked up again when they fell, Charles agreed, but he still saw heavy walls running steeply uphill, up the mountain, where there were larks and where the bleating of sheep sounded sharply. If the bleating were sharp, the fleeces were soft, heavy, wet, and the heather was wet, brittle heather, wet with mist or with dew. In the walls there grew minute ferns, and Charles saw them minutely—with a minuteness he had not seen for years, finger-length ferns that curled round your fingers. One ought to have time to see minute things minutely.

"Charles."

Where was it? Charles groped for his wall. Where had he seen it? Scotland? Cornwall? Wales?

"Charles."

Wales!

"Charles! I have called you three times. It's time for the news."

He opened his eyes. "Who was that girl I met on the stairs?" he asked before he switched on the television.

Sophie looked at him. "You know very well who she is."

"If I did, I shouldn't ask you," said Charles with exemplary patience.

"How odd you are tonight." "Odd" was one of Sophie's words; with her it meant unlike herself. "You knew she was coming. Why, we advertised, wrote and discussed the whole thing, and decided . . ."

"Oh! The Welsh girl. Now I see. The mother's help. I see," said Charles more slowly, and he seemed to see the girl again. After a moment he said, "She doesn't look like a mother's help."

"She doesn't behave like one either," said Sophie. "She's so cool. I don't mean impudent. I mean . . ." She searched for the word and gave it up. "Cool," she said helplessly. "She talks as if she were . . . at home with you, but it's not personal. That is what makes it so disconcerting, as if she were at home with everything, and yet she's an ignorant girl, brought up on a farm, far far away . . ."

"Yes," said Charles, "with mist and the sheep and heather and grey walls." Now he knew why these things had been in his mind; was it premonition, telepathy? He saw the girl again as he had seen her last night on the stairs; she was a thin, dark girl, but he had an impression of glimmers of whiteness, like those rifts in my mind, he thought; her white neck under the dark hair, her old-fashioned white apron.

"Good evening," he had said.

"Good evening, Mr. Carne."

Again Sophie was right. The girl seemed at home; her voice was level, her smile grave, as if she knew exactly what she had to do; she was interested in him as equally as she was interested in everything else. "Good evening, Mr. Carne," he murmured.

"What did you say, Charles?"

"I was wondering . . ." said Charles, but he was not talking to Sophie, he was thinking aloud.

"Wondering what?"

"If that is her strength. Her power."

"She doesn't look strong to me," said Sophie. "She's too thin. She's odd," said Sophie. "Her name is Gwyneth Lloyd Jones."

"That isn't odd if you're Welsh," said Charles.

Sophie woke Charles in the night. "You keep kicking and talking. Are you dreaming?"

"Yes. I was dreaming," said Charles, "of earth and walls, granite walls."

"Walls again," Sophie yawned. "There's no granite here."

"There's nothing here that comes out of the earth," said Charles contemptuously. "Nothing. Everything is brought here . . . in lorries."

"Oh, Charles! Do be quiet and go to sleep."

He slept then until Gwyneth knocked and brought in the morning tea; at once he was wide awake, sensitive again and thought, from the way she put down the tray, that she felt it strange that two people should choose to lie in bed and have tea brought them by another.

"She's very *farouche,* isn't she?" said Sophie.

"Yes," said Charles. He did not want to discuss Gwyneth.

Now that Gwyneth had come, Sophie decided to breakfast in bed. "I deserve a rest," she said. For months they had been without anyone and, "This is luxury," said Sophie. Charles had breakfast in the dining-room and Gwyneth gave Patrick his in the kitchen. Gwyneth handed Charles his coffee and porridge and bacon and toast through the hatch and he knew she wondered why they could not have breakfasted more simply and directly together.

After a week he began to talk to her. "You're never late, Gwyneth, but I never hear your alarm."

"I haven't a clock. I wake," said Gwyneth.

"But when?"

"When it's morning."

"Yes, but when is it morning?"

"When—when you wake," and she said, "Living on a farm, you learn to wake early."

"You were brought up on a farm?"

"Yes, Mr. Carne."

"A sheep farm? On the mountain? With a grey house and heather, and larks and blackberries, and lots of rain and mist and mud?"

"All that," said Gwyneth with her smile.

"And summer-time? And double summer-time?"

"That's wicked," said Gwyneth with a sudden flash. "Wicked for the animals, and the farmers, and the children."

"You must change and learn new ways."

"The sun won't learn," flashed Gwyneth. "Nor land, nor crops. How will you work your day when you can't start cutting till twelve o'clock because the dew isn't off the hay? When the hens won't be ready to be shut up till ten or eleven at night?"

"But you must live in the world as it is, Gwyneth."

"That isn't the world as it is," said Gwyneth with scorn. Charles had a suspicion, almost amounting to certainty, that she was right.

Charles liked to hear her talking to Patrick in the kitchen. Patrick was his son who, unlike Gwyneth, was being carefully trained in the way of the present world: time to get up, time for walk: lunch time, tea time, time for school, time for reading, time for bed. Now it occurred to Charles to wonder if Patrick had ever had a day, a whole day, unchopped by rules and times, for himself.

"Tell about fishing," he would urge Gwyneth.

"I've told you."

"Tell me again."

"We used to go off fishing," Gwyneth was telling Patrick, "with bread and jam in our pockets."

"And when did you come back?" asked Patrick.

"When we came back," said Gwyneth.

"And you had no shoes . . ." Patrick was enthralled.

"Of course we had shoes. Eat up your cereal."

"But you didn't wear them," said Patrick, triumphantly. "You tied the laces together and hung them round your necks, but didn't you get pricks?"

"No, because our feet were hard," said Gwyneth. "We went over the rocks and stones and in and out of the streams."

"I want to have no shoes," cried Patrick.

"You can't in a town."

"But I want to. I will! I will!" cried Patrick, but of course he would not, not until it was time to go to the seaside. Perhaps he sensed that. He said angrily, "I shall run away."

"Eat up your cereal, love," said Gwyneth.

Behind the houses there was a hill that had been left with its beechwoods and its bracken when the lower ground was cleared for the desirable suburb. On the hill behind the trees one could not see the houses, only hear the station and the church clocks, and measure time by the bus that ran up and down to the foot of the hill. Gwyneth took Patrick there on Saturdays for an afternoon walk, though Sophie said it was too cold in winter. "We scamper," said Gwyneth, laughing. One Saturday afternoon Charles said he wanted to walk there too.

"I don't know why you want to. The woods are damp and cold and the trees are still bare," said Sophie.

"I like them bare."

"You are odd," said Sophie. "Well, I want to finish my book. You go. Gwyneth and Patrick have gone already. Please be back in time for tea."

Charles lit his pipe and walked up the hill.

There was a place in the woods below the rounded crest of the hill where, looking up through the beech trees, through trunks and boles and stems and branches, he saw the sky above the rising of the hill; the woods looked as if they rolled for ever, on into a forest perhaps, then, ceasing to be forest, turned to common and plain, and returned to the woods, to forests, back to plain, on and on to mountains and the sea. That is what it was like before we interrupted it, thought Charles. We men, building like ants. At first the buildings had not been an interruption but an outcome of the earth itself; only steadings and walls and farms; a keep, a castle, small towns, turrets of churches, and churchyards where the graves took the bodies quietly back into the earth. Men lived on the earth then, said Charles—but he was talking to himself because no one else would understand—with earth, for it, and ended in it: it was like a pageant, he thought, a home-made pageant, not acted but lived. Now it was gone, or we are gone far, far off, thought Charles, and partly because he was so tired, he sighed.

Then he saw Patrick and Gwyneth coming down the hill. Patrick had toadstools, a sprig of blackthorn, and a cocoon, though it was a dead one. "But the blackthorn is alive," said Patrick, "and there'll be much more soon." He was red-cheeked, and excited by the winter afternoon, he went hurtling down the hill, running all ways, and tumbling down, rolling and getting up again: Charles felt himself stirring too, though he did not want to run. Gwyneth waited, standing in her grey coat, looking away from him, up through the beech trees.

Suddenly there was a whirring sound, filling the air, over the trees, the sound of scores and scores of wings.

"Near four o'clock," said Gwyneth certainly, "time to go in."

"How do you know?"

"Those were starlings. They fly near four o'clock."

Charles looked at his watch. It was ten minutes past four.

The flight had passed, the air was still, but the sound of the wings was still beating in him. He immediately began to explain it to himself. Of course. They fly before dusk. That is when they would fly. That is quite reasonable, and he asked Gwyneth, "But if it were summer?"

"It would be nearer seven," said Gwyneth. She smiled. "But it would still be time to go in."

Charles turned away from her. He could bear his tiredness and dissatisfaction no longer; it was more than dissatisfaction, it was dismay; it was more than dismay, it was panic. Panic! He was lonely, remote, lost, without life. Yes, I am lost, lost, cried Charles silently, bitterly. I have been lost for a long, long time. For all of my life, cried Charles. I have never had life, and he did not know how he could find himself, how live; he did not know, but this terrible sense of loss swept through him as the flight of starlings had swept over the wood. He could have thrown himself down on the ground in his despair and wept, only that the ground, of course, was damp and he could not weep in front of Gwyneth.

Gwyneth!

Charles looked at her. She was waiting for him, standing in her grey coat against the tree, not thinking of him very much perhaps, but according him her usual courtesy. Behind her the trees rose up to the hill, as if they were rolling away, thought Charles, on and on and on, and calmness and clarity came into his mind. Steadings, walls, farms, keeps, thought Charles. Fields and graves and churches. Forests and common and plain and mountains. A mountain had mist, heather, sheep. They seemed, peculiarly, to belong to him and now they were not far away; he could see the wall, he could even see the ferns in the wall, and he said aloud, with a curious urge to say it, "Gwyneth, let me go with you to your farm."

"To the farm, Mr. Carne?"

As soon as he said it he had been horribly afraid of her surprise, but there was no surprise in Gwyneth. She looked at him gravely, quietly, as if she agreed with him. "Yes, it's good there, on the farm," she said, but as she said it, Charles knew she saw no possibility of it for him, any more than she saw, seriously, Patrick's running away. I'm serious; but he had not the courage to say it aloud.

It was growing dark in the wood. The outline of the hill was blurred; it had lost its distance, and at the same time its nearness to Charles. "No," he cried. "No!"

Then the station clock struck from the town and the church clocks after it and they heard the bus start up in the road. "A quarter past four," said Charles and looked at his watch. "Time for tea."

Gwyneth smiled at him and turned to go home. Her grey coat hardly showed in the dusk, but when she had faced him, her hands and neck and face had glimmered pale, white, as he first remembered them. Now, as she turned her back to him, he could not see her at all.

"Gwyneth!" he thought he called, but she did not turn so he could have made no sound. He hit the bracken with his stick. There was no response. The bracken did not even wilt. "Hell!" said Charles and started down the hill.

❧

Lily and the Sparrows

❦

Though a short story is not often the forerunner of a book, this has happened with me several times, and "Lily and the Sparrows" was, I suppose, a first—or "bud"—attempt to write about the cockney children of my novel *An Episode of Sparrows*.

I have had many periods of living in London, sometimes for a few weeks or months, once for five years, and it is the place where I should choose to live if I were completely free. I love the city streets, the constant life, and most of all, the way one can be "a fly on the wall," totally unnoticed; in London I found I could study these children, listen to them, and leave them unaware. For them I could disappear into a park bench, a seat on a bus, behind the newspaper I was pretending to read while I stood on the pavement or outside a school playground. No one noticed, but then in London no one cares how peculiar you look, how oddly you behave; it is full of oddities.

I nicknamed the children "sparrows" because outside school hours they were always in the street, and because of the anonymous noise like chirping that used to rise up from the playground five streets away, as soon as there was "break" or the children were let out of school. At one time I had a tiny cottage in a mews tucked away at the back of a line of stately houses, like the one Miss Mantle looked after in the London Square. The children used to congregate in the mews to play the games that came round in season as inexorably as the months of the year; the paving stones outside my cottage made a level place for hopscotch or skipping or conkers or football, so that I was able to watch and eavesdrop at ground level; as I sat in my window on the low window-seat my head was often no higher than the children's, so that I could see from their perspective—a great advantage for a writer.

"Lily and the Sparrows" is a cruel story. Children are said to be cruel and bloodthirsty; individually I have found they seldom are, but they are terribly susceptible—and I mean terribly—to mob or gang psychology. We all know that mob emotion can make quite kind ordinary adults behave like harpies or drunks; it can turn children into monsters.

Lily and the Sparrows

❦   ❦   ❦

Miss Mantle was the caretaker at the big corner house, and the voices of the children, playing in the back street behind it, came up to her room like the sound of sparrows.

The children could, of course, have played in the square garden that had, nowadays, no railings; it was graciously planted with plane trees and the peculiarly vivid green of London grass, but they preferred to play in the bylane, the mean little street that still had its cobbles.

"Well, I like my tea in my own brown teapot," said Miss Mantle, who could at any time have used a silver teapot or a Spode. "We know what we feel at home with, me and the sparrows."

She called them the sparrows, perhaps because that was the best aspect she could give them. Truth to tell she did not like them very much. They were not attractive children: London weeds, with pale faces and pale knobbed arms and legs, then kneecaps and elbows and knuckles and eyes too big for their size. A few were Jewish, paler and darker than the others, and one had auburn hair and an elderly sharp face that seemed a pointer in expression to them all. Her name, Miss Mantle thought, must have been Kitty; they called her Mew.

Some were clean and some dirty, but they were all shabby on weekdays and smart on Sunday, and they were all noisy; the little boys had scooters, the middling ones roller-skates, and the big boys, some as big as fourteen, had steel tips to their shoes. They used twanging cinema words and they could leave nothing alone; if they saw a tin they must kick it, a poster they must deface it, a fly they must catch it, and they went on at each other, twisting, scuffling, calling, plotting, wrestling, whispering with an unremitting strength that horrified Miss Mantle if she went too near them; but up in her room, their voices sounded like sparrows.

From high up their voices, coming up to Miss Mantle, were oddly touching; they made only a twitter in the air; in its blueness, its sun or grey, all their human harmfulness and wilfulness was lost. "And if sparrows peck and fight, it is small," said Miss Mantle. In some ways it comforted her to think how small it was.

The little girl with the auburn hair, Mew, was persistent. Unlike the others, she was curious about the great house at whose back they played, and even more than the others, she could leave nothing untouched or alone. She began to waylay Miss Mantle; she watched for her to take in the milk; she met her on her way to do her shopping, and she pestered to be shown the rooms inside. Miss Mantle did not want to, she did not mean to, but her strength was no match for Mew's and she let her in; but that was not enough. Mew had to handle and finger everything. It cost Miss Mantle a great effort to get rid of the child.

Miss Mantle spent all her time in the vast empty house. She was there to wash the marble of its entrance floors, the columns of its fireplaces, to keep its paint, and go over the carpets with the electric cleaner; to unshroud the chairs and sofas and cover them up again, and dust the piled-up stacks of china and pictures. She went out only to the baker and grocer and butcher; for the rest she worked in the house and lived in her one back room.

"You are too lonely, Mantle," said her lady on one of her visits to town. "Haven't you any nieces who could come and live with you?"

"No, no nieces, Madam," said Miss Mantle, "no one at all."

"Well, I shall get you a dog."

"A—dog, Madam?" said Miss Mantle faintly.

"Yes, a dear little dog. That will be company." And next time she came she brought a dog so small that it would have gone inside a muff; compact, silky, and gay, and as white as pearls or barley or new milk teeth.

"Oh—Madam!" said Miss Mantle.

"She's white and she's Chinese," said her lady, laughing. "You must call her Shanghai Lil." That was too difficult for Miss Mantle. She called her Lily.

How could one dog, as small as that, fill an empty mansion, its presence run a cord through an adult life, pulling it into shape, giving it life and meaning, sense and wit, fine wits, fine senses, that Miss Mantle had scarcely known she possessed? Perhaps it was because Lily herself possessed them in such great degree; all her wits and all her senses were incarnate in the springs of her little body: firm bones, sound flesh, busy pads, glistening fur, and round bright eyes. Lily had abundant life and abundant mischief, and to Miss Mantle, who had dealt so long with inanimate things, her animation was the wonder. It took her all her time to keep up with Lily; she had to move quickly and be agile. Lily needed meals promptly cooked and so she cooked them for herself as well. Lily needed to go out into the Square, and as she could not go alone, Miss Mantle went too. As Lily grew larger, though she never grew very large, her inquisitiveness grew larger too and she wanted to go farther; soon they were going for walks. Strangers in the streets and in the parks stopped to admire Lily, and pride, a thing she had hardly felt before, woke in Miss Mantle; she bought a sealskin coat, new shoes, a velvet hat like a toque, and every Sunday she brushed Lily with especial care, then dressed herself and out they went to the Park. When they came in they had a toasted muffin; Lily one-eighth, Miss Mantle seven-eighths; then they sat by the fire and the voices of the sparrows, less sharp, more idle and released on Sundays, came up to the window, but Lily was too replete and well exercised to move. Presently, late in the evening when the sparrows went in, quiet settled in the room like snow, and the fire shed a glow that reddened Lily's sleeping fur to ruby.

On weekdays, as soon as she heard the sparrows, Lily would run to the door. It was the one thing that disappointed Miss Mantle, Lily's predilection for the sparrows; as soon as she heard their voices she demanded to be let out. "No, you can't play with them. They are too rough and strong for you," but it was plain that Lily did not care how rough and strong they were, they were young and she wanted to play. It hurt Miss Mantle to think that she was too old and stiff and slow to satisfy Lily, but it was true; as well expect a fairy to play with a seal—Miss Mantle felt she looked like an old black seal in her sealskin coat. Against her better judgment she asked Mew in to play with Lily.

Mew was able to get down on her hands and knees and pounce out on Lily as Lily pounced on her; round and round the great dining-room table they went. Mew could laugh so lightly that it sounded to Miss Mantle like the expression of Lily, as Lily would have laughed had she been a child. Almost Miss Mantle's heart softened towards Mew, but it soon hardened again.

As soon as Mew set eyes on Lily she wanted to take her out.

"Jus' as far as the Post Office!"

"No."

"Jus' round the Square!"

"No."

"To show my Mum. Jus' my Mum."

"No."

"Oh, you might! Jus' let Bob and Alfie see her. Alfie's my brother. Please!"

"No."

"For a teeny-weeny second. Jus' Bob and Alfie."

"Bob and Alfie are far too rough for her."

"They wouldn't hurt her. They're not bad kids really. They get excited but they don't mean nothin'. I'll be ever s'careful. Please, Miss Mantle."

"No," said Miss Mantle. She felt as if she were fighting for breath and she knew, from the look on Mew's sharp face, that she meant to take Lily.

"Tell you a secret," said Mew to Lily, and she whispered in Lily's ear. "Tell you a secret." Miss Mantle had the distinct thought that Lily listened, and she had a spasm of such forlornness that she was startled. "Lily, Lily," she said helplessly, "you don't know what you're doing," and as she began to dust a Dresden dessert service, its painted plates felt heavy in her hand.

One afternoon Miss Mantle went up to her room, leaving Mew downstairs with Lily. Mew had just come in from school and they were playing; a staybone had worked through its cover and was cutting Miss Mantle under her breast. She went to her room.

As she came in at the door she heard the sparrows and went to the window to look at them. The little boys had their scooters; one very small boy, with dark curls, sat on a doorstep with a hearth-broom and a toy iron wheelbarrow beside him. A little girl was pulling another little girl along in a truck, but the truck was so small that when it met a high cobble the smaller girl was thrown up in the air and landed, sitting behind it, on the cobbles.

"Fancy!" said Miss Mantle, "and in she gets again. Fancy!" The big boys were kicking a tin about, trying to play football. The tin was too light and it rattled. Seems as if someone ought to give them a ball, thought Miss Mantle. That afternoon the sparrows seemed to her disarming. She stood looking down on them almost tenderly before she turned away to tussle with the staybone.

It would not come out. Miss Mantle grew quite red in the face and out of breath and oblivious to anything but the obstinate bone. A gay little yelp made her stop; she listened and pulled down her dress and ran to the window.

In the middle of a ring of children she saw Lily. Lily was slightly frightened, her tail was nearly down. Behind her stood Mew making important gesticulations. Fury filled Miss Mantle. She threw up the window and called, "Mew! Mew!" No one heard her. Their voices came up shrill to her but they could not hear hers. Even the little ones had left their play and come to look.

Lily stood in the centre of them and she was ceasing to be frightened. She was growing pleased. She looked tiny among all their feet and legs. Miss Mantle called again. "Mew! Boys! Mew! Bring Lily back at once. Mew! Mew!" She might not have called at all, for all it reached them. No one looked up or moved. Miss Mantle tried to whistle but her lips were dry. She knew how long it would take her to go down through the house and round by the street. "Mew!" she called, "Mew!"

As Lily grew more pleased she began to pounce out on the children from behind their legs. They laughed and her eyes grew wild with pleasure, her ears and tail danced. They laughed louder with surprise and delight.

"Look at her. Look at her."

"Coo! Isn' she sweet!"

"Look at 'er, Charlie. See that!"

Mew hopped up and down and shrilled, "Didn' I tell you!" and somebody cried out, "She's like a ball."

Miss Mantle leaned against the window. Her strength ebbed away.

One of the boys put out his foot and touched Lily with his shoe. She bounced off it and bounced back. He lifted her a little way and passed her to the boy called Charlie. Charlie called "Bob!" and pushed her to him. Lily lost her balance and fell on her side, scuffling along the ground. She gave a yelp, not gay but astonished.

"Don't, Charlie," cried Mew. "You're making her all dirty. Don't."

"Do her good, little sissy-pants," cried Charlie and everyone laughed, and he pushed her neatly to Bob. Lily was offended and turned round and round. They laughed more. She was growing bewildered and very dirty.

Then Mew's red-headed brother Alfie gave Lily a small, real kick. He did not mean it to be hard but the steel tip of his shoe caught her mouth and made it bleed. Alfie looked aghast. Mew screamed and Charlie called, "Look out, you sod! That's too hard." Alfie turned sulky and picked Lily up. Mew tugged him, trying to get Lily away, and Alfie broke her hold and ran down the street. "Oh, get him! Get him!" cried Mew. "Go after him. Oh, get him!" Bob and Charlie started after him and Alfie began to twist and dodge as if he were playing and Lily was really a ball. Their shoes slipped on the cobbles, they were out of breath and laughing and when Bob caught Alfie by the collar, they fell helplessly on the ground. Blood from Lily's mouth spurted over them both as she came down smack on the cobbles underneath them. They could not get up because Charlie, laughing still, fell on top of them. Then other boys came running, someone called, "He's got the ball," and there was a mess of arms and legs and threshing shoes and butting heads, and suddenly, because of the smell of blood and the heat of their pressed-up bodies, something more heady than laughter came into them and they began to fight. They clinched and kicked and gave near hard blows with their fists, with grunts and swear-words; there was not a sound from the girls who stood transfixed with horror round them, and not a sound from Lily, but Miss Mantle made a strange noise, a plummet falling down and down and down as she stood, pressed against the window with her hands on the glass and her eyes closed.

It was Mew's father who brought Lily back, what was left of Lily: a crushed handful of soot and blood and fur. "I don't know what you can do with this," he said, "but I thought I better bring her. I—I would give those kids a hiding, if I thought it would do any good—give one to young Mew too. Think I will. Don't know what to say, Miss."

Miss Mantle said nothing at all. She took the still handful that was Lily and held it to her breast against her apron. "They didn't mean it. That's about all you can say," said Mew's father. "They didn't know what they was doin'. You mustn' think that. Not bad kids really."

It was later that Miss Mantle went up to her room. She knew she would soon have to feel something. Better not to think about Lily. Lily was gone and with Lily was gone her new life. "It wasn't mine. Only lent—lent," said Miss Mantle and immediately, fiercely, she knew it was hers, as Lily had been, and now it was torn away and killed. The pain was unbearable but soon, mercifully, it grew dull.

From habit she went to the window. It was evening, still playtime, but the street below was subdued, almost empty. Only the little ones were there. Running her thumb along a crack in the sill, she wondered if the father had beaten Mew. She wondered about black eyes, cut lips, bruises, and broken collar bones. "No, they didn't think what they were doing," whispered Miss Mantle.

She thought about the sparrows, those sparrows in the street, and she found that she was trying to think of something comforting for them, though why she should comfort the sparrows she could not tell. "There is something," whispered Miss Mantle, "something that someone once said." She was too tired to think of it but she wanted to say it. "Something that was for them, on purpose for them."

She watched the last light grow richer and deeper as it left the street. "Not a hair of their heads . . . ?" But sparrows did

not have hair, only cheeky cockney feathers. Or was it of falling, of sparrows that fall? Bob on top of Alfie and Charlie on
Bob and more and more and more . . . Then the words were
torn from her, the right words, that comforted: "Father, forgive the sparrows for they don't know what they do."

❧

To Uncle, with Love

In our family, Christmas was a thoroughly kept festival and brought an adamantine necessity of present-giving that was hard on us four small girls at the tail of the family clan. Parcels came from our Worcestershire relations, from relations in Taunton and London, and most sent individual presents, necessitating a return. Aunt Gertrude, for instance, would send, besides three bottles of sherry for our parents, four pretty packets for us. Long before the days of gay packing papers Aunt Gertrude painted roses on her white papers and tied the packets with green and pink ribbons that were slightly scented as if Aunt Gertrude herself were inside. They were so pretty that we longed to send something worthy to her; we worked hard but our prospects were meagre. "It's the thought that counts," our nearest aunt, Aunt Hilda, would say, but to be any use at Christmas the smallest thought had to be embodied—and our pocket-money was only ninepence a week each.

For weeks before Christmas we toiled at bookmarkers, penwipers, raffia table-napkin rings, calendars. The uncles were particularly difficult. Our little sisters had a monopoly, protected by our mother, Mam, of the two things we could make easily and cheaply: one was spills, the other an improbable looking thing called a shaving ball made of rosettes twisted out of paper; the uncle was supposed to pull a rosette off each morning and wipe his razor on it to save cutting the towels. "You two big ones must think of your own ideas," said Mam.

"Yes, Mam," we said and sighed.

Of all the uncles, our Uncle Edward was the most difficult. Perhaps even then we realized dimly that he had something that was missing from the other uncles and aunts—except perhaps Aunt Gertrude—something not to be ignored, that lingered. I know now that it was quality.

He was our eldest maternal uncle and as English as his name, Edward; his essence was a mildness that held an unruffled strength, and his life had flowed, because he had so made it flow, with the steady untroubled peace of one of our English rivers.

Each weekday morning he left the house by taxi—the same taxi—for the office (he kept his old-fashioned, snub-nosed, two-seater Morris Cowley for weekends and holidays). He was a partner in a firm of solicitors in our seaside town and I can remember his office, full of black tin deed boxes, his desk piled with documents, but its very air deliberate and serene. Every day he lunched at the same table in the restaurant at Boots, the chemist. His friends and colleagues lunched at the Royal Sussex Hotel, but there the wine waiter came round and asked, embarrassingly, for orders and my Uncle Edward did not drink. At five o'clock he left the office and took the bus to the corner of his road where he walked up the chalky lane to his house. He was a bachelor and lived with his maiden sister, my Aunt Hilda, on the edge of the rolling green Sussex hills. The house was small but the garden was large and he spent every available moment working in it. As soon as he came in, he changed into a disgraceful tattered Burberry and an old green hat and gardened. At seven o'clock Aunt Hilda called him and they had supper; after supper he sat by the dining-room fire and read the *Times* or *Punch* while my aunt retired to the drawing-room. At nine o'clock he went in to her and they talked a little and had tea. At ten he wound the clocks, shut the house, and went to bed.

Little else happened. Occasionally he watched cricket—the town had a famous cricket ground—and once a year he stayed a few days with his brother in Worcestershire. Every spring he was moved to get out the Morris Cowley and spend whole days in the country; he went to see the poetry of bluebells and wild cherries in the woods and drove by farmhouses with their red-brown Sussex tiled roofs standing in what we, Worcestershire bred, called a blow of apple blossoms. Every autumn he saw the bracken turn in Ashdown Forest and he still kept the canoe he had had at Oxford; now it was paddled on the Little Ouse, a tiny placid river that wound through meadows of buttercups and under tangles of wild roses where the swans floated in the shade.

Uncle Edward's things were curiously elegant for a country solicitor. The canoe, Dream Days, was fitted with velvet cushions in yellow and had monogrammed paddles; Uncle Edward's books had special bindings, his slippers, his handkerchiefs, his pipe, his tobacco, were unusually good. How could we give him a lead pencil, a packet of drawing-pins, a cake of cheap soap, which was all our money would run to? Every year we asked ourselves that question, but the Christmas I was twelve years old, the position was particularly acute; I found myself with only threepence to spend on Uncle Edward.

"Give him a card," said Ruth, who was happily furnished

with a comb-case she had made; but cards were considered paltry and all presents were distributed with horrible publicity from the tree in Aunt Hilda's drawing-room.

Aunt Hilda, in real life, did what the maiden aunt of a family is supposed to do in novels; she kept count of all the family threads and wove them tightly together. There were many threads and all of them, or as many as possible, were gathered into one knot for Christmas.

"Nothing for Uncle Edward!" Aunt Hilda would say, and at four o'clock on that Christmas Eve I had nothing.

We, Ruth and I, were standing outside Fidler's bookshop in the South Parade and I was turning over a tray of second-hand books marked "All at 3d." It was the 3d that had attracted me, not the books; they were shabby and dirty and at no moment had I thought of giving Uncle Edward a book. Books were of grown-ups' bestowing. We had been shopping all afternoon and were tired and hungry.

"I'm going home to tea," said Ruth.

"I can't till I've found him a present," I said.

I watched Ruth, in her brown school coat and brown soup-plate hat, go up the street. She grew smaller and smaller until she went quite out of sight. My feet were cold, I was miserable with worry; listlessly I turned over the books, and then I saw it.

It was under the tray, under a sheet of newspaper as well; I wonder now if it had been put there for someone to come and fetch quietly away. Lifting the newspaper I caught sight of its cover, which was of clean white vellum stamped in gold. It was a book that looked not unlike some of Uncle Edward's own books and I could not imagine how it came to be in the 3d tray, but cautiously I drew it out, opened it, and took a quick look inside. It was poems with a few pictures, and it was obviously quite new; most of the pages were uncut. I felt the endpapers, which were of satiny white paper stamped with a curious little object in gold that conveyed nothing to me at all, nor did the title that I made out with difficulty, "Sonnets on the Kama Sutra." I could not stop to read or look very carefully and in any case I was stunned by the beauty of the binding and paper. I could hardly believe my luck.

The custom at Fidler's, for a buyer from the cheap trays, was to take the book of his choice and leave the money in a saucer set on the tray; at that price one could not expect the attention of a bookseller. I had an uneasy feeling that I should have gone in and asked Mr. Fidler about this book but, "It was in the threepenny tray," I said stoutly to Ruth afterwards and I dropped my threepence in the saucer, put the book under my coat and ran all the way home.

I showed the book to Ruth but there was no time to do more than glance at it, because Mam was waiting for us to take our presents up to Aunt Hilda's and hang them on the tree for the Christmas afternoon party.

"Do it up," urged Ruth.

"There's a picture of a naked woman and man in the front," I said. I had just seen it and it made me hesitate.

"They are probably gods," said Ruth. Gods, we knew, were allowed to be naked as long as their hands were properly disposed.

Then I saw there was a sub-title and read it aloud. "Kama Sutra. The Eight Attitudes and Sixty-four Ingredients of Love." It sounded strange; I had not known that love had attitudes or ingredients. *"Will* it do for Uncle Edward?" I asked, hesitating still more.

"Well, Mam says he is the most loving man we know," said Ruth, "and it looks quite new. Hurry. Do it up."

Uncle Edward opened my parcel almost at the last. I was covertly watching. He undid the string, opened the paper and looked. After a moment I began to think he was stunned himself, he was so still. I took this as a tribute; it was a surprisingly handsome book to come from an obscure niece. He opened the front cover, still keeping the book in its paper, not once did he lift it proudly out to public view as I had hoped; I had written a card, "To Uncle, with love," with my name underneath and he shot a look in my direction. Then I saw that he had coloured deeply—with pleasure? I wonder—and all at once I was as uncertain as I had been when I saw the naked gods. The next minute he had wrapped it swiftly up again and thrust it under all his other present and, his fingers trembling a little, began to undo José's packet of spills.

He had been quick, but not quick enough for Aunt Alice. "Why, what have you got there?" she asked.

"Nothing," said Uncle with strange briefness.

Nothing! My precious book! I opened my mouth but I got a look from my uncle that I had never had before, a look that quelled me.

"But I saw . . ." said Aunt Hilda.

"It's a book of poems," said Uncle. "They are only for me."

"You funny girl," said Aunt Hilda, who had caught sight of my card and immediately thought I had written them. "Poems! Uncle doesn't go in for that sort of thing at all."

There was a sudden sound from Uncle Edward. "What's the matter, Edward?" asked Aunt Hilda. I raised my head and looked at him. He was quietly opening his presents but it had sounded like—a chuckle?

Three days after the funeral Aunt Hilda began to cry; she had been quietly through it all, the death, the cremation that was done by Uncle's wish, the return to the empty house, the reading of the will, and the task we were busy with at present, the sorting of his things. I had come to help Aunt Hilda and Mam with that. Now we were at tea and I had said something a little inarticulate about Uncle Edward and teas in other times, about his gentleness and goodness. Aunt Hilda had burst into tears, tears that were inexplicable from her because they were bitter.

"I should rather have cut off my hand than have to know this," she sobbed, and when we asked what "this" was, she could only sob, "Edward! Edward of all people, to do *that*!"

"Do *what*, Aunt Hilda?"

"I never meant to tell anyone but I can't keep it to myself," she sobbed. "Edward, whom I could have sworn . . . I know some men are nasty but not Edward!"

"Nasty?" Mam and I said together, "Uncle *Edward* nasty?"

"Like dirty postcards!" and Aunt Hilda wept again.

"Aunt Hilda," I said firmly, "do please tell us what you are talking about."

She sat up and dabbed her eyes and then said in a quick, stifled voice, "Edward kept pornographic books in his drawer —a pornographic book."

"Edward?" "Uncle Edward?" We were both stupefied. Then, "Are you *sure*?" I asked, but Aunt Hilda stood up, tears spattering on her blouse, and went across the room to his desk;

it was a knee-hole desk and on the right-hand side was a deep drawer; it was locked; she took a key, unlocked the drawer, and opened it.

When I looked in I had tears in my own eyes. I had not known that Uncle had really cared for us, but in the drawer were all the presents we children had given him, carefully dated and labelled; home-drawn cards and clumsy spills, a pair of knitted scarlet cuffs sewn crooked, blotters and calendars, pen-wipers, table-napkin rings, unused shaving balls! "I always knew those things were no use," I said unsteadily, touching the dusty rosettes with my finger.

"He thought a lot of you children," said Mam.

"That's what makes it so much worse," said Aunt Hilda, and her tears ran over again. "Look," she said, and as if it were red hot, from underneath everything else, as he had once hidden it under his parcels, she pulled out a book. I recognized it instantly: "Kama Sutra. The Eight Attitudes and Sixty-four Ingredients of Love."

"But I gave him that," I said.

"*You!*" She and Mam stared at me appalled.

"Yes. Look." The book was as new as when I had bought it, its pages were still uncut and my card was where I had put it. "To Uncle, with love." "Don't you remember . . . ?" I said.

"But—you nasty child!" Aunt Hilda's voice began to rise.

"I was only twelve," I pleaded but, looking at the book, I wondered that even then I had not guessed what it was; I looked at the endpapers with their frank phallic design, the front picture—gods indeed!—at the first lines of a poem; I was a mature, grown woman but I grew hot as I looked and I stood before Aunt Hilda as ashamed as I should have been if Uncle had uncovered it that day. "I didn't know what it was," I said, "I was only twelve."

"Twelve or not!" snapped Aunt Hilda.

"It was Christmas . . . "

I stopped. Aunt Hilda paused. We seemed to hear something, something I thought I had heard on that Christmas day long ago: Uncle Edward's chuckle.

We looked at one another and began to laugh.

Fireworks for Elspeth

❦

"Why," asked the young man from the B.B.C. "do you write so much about nuns?"

I did not know that I wrote "much about" them; *Black Narcissus,* which was about an active order in the Himalayas in India, was published nearly thirty years ago, while this short story was written in 1952.

The war and several books intervened between the two. It is true that the novel I am working on now is a study of the contemplative life, but that will not be published for a year or more, may in fact never be published because a book can always fail and writing about nuns is exceedingly difficult—if they are to be true nuns (so often in books their stories are distorted). To make a true nun, with true ideals, convincing to the public is, to borrow a phrase from Dom Hubert van Zeller, himself a gifted writer, "as if a fish were trying to explain the merits of water to a bird or a happy drunkard."

Perhaps that young interviewer had fathomed the fact that I have always been interested in nuns, even fascinated by them; theirs seems to me to be a love story that transcends all ordinary love stories, yet the strange part is that this fascination began as dislike, even hate. "When I am a grown writer," I used to promise myself at my convent school—shown as St. Monica's in "The Little Fishes"—"when I'm a real writer, I shall write a book about nuns and tell what they are really like!" It was a desire for revenge, for the misery they caused me, for the worse way they treated my sister Jon, but when I began to write *Black Narcissus* and had to think more deeply about religious life, the hate, and most of the dislike, disappeared.

"Fireworks for Elspeth" is not founded on one happening, but thousands of them; behind every nun lies a story and usually, a struggle; that moment of leaving home, of renunciation, has always seemed to me poignant and filled with drama and meaning. I hope a little of those qualities have found their way into the story.

Fireworks for Elspeth

❦ ❦ ❦

When Elspeth woke on the last morning, she was visited by a feeling of extraordinary simplicity; everything she had to do was done; there was nothing now but to go. She felt as if the doors and windows of the house were already wide open, with the sun shining on its white walls, on the lawns and the lavender bushes; the sun seemed to make a path from her own window over the lawn and the tops of the trees, over the copse to the wood and the sky; yes, it looked like a path. I have only to go, thought Elspeth blissfully. Roderick, her black cocker spaniel, lay at the foot of her bed; there was, it was true, a gap in her mind where she must say good-bye to Roderick—but that was legitimate grief, thought Elspeth, nothing disturbing. Nothing disturbing, she thought and stretched herself on the bed; then she remembered the lunch party.

How she had pleaded with Mother! "A lunch party! Oh, *Mother*, no! Please no."

"Why not?"

"It wouldn't be—suitable," Elspeth had said, with temerity.

"Elspeth, do I or do I not know what is suitable?"

"*Not* a party!"

"Just the family and a few intimate friends."

"But they are the worst."

"Elspeth!"

Elspeth would have liked to have said, it's the questions and the looks. I feel the looks, Mother. I know I shouldn't feel them but—but I do and they talk so much. They—they prise everything open. Aunt Euphrosyne and Morna and Jean, Lady Bannerman, all of them. They know me so well they take it for granted they can ask things but . . . they have such picking eyes, thought Elspeth in despair. They pick everything to pieces, into little, little pieces; this is whole, in me, but they tatter it to pieces. I know it is my fault to let them, but they do. "Mother," she had begun aloud but Mother was saying, "Just Aunt Euphrosyne and Uncle Arthur and Morna and Jean. Major Fitzgerald, of course . . ."

"And the Baldocks and Lady Bannerman and Larry and Colin Crump," said Elspeth bitterly.

"They are exactly whom I thought of asking," said Mother; then she had looked at Elspeth and her face hardened. "Well, Elspeth, why not?"

Elspeth could never say things to Mother; she could have talked to Aunt Bevis but that would have made Mother worse. "Bevis is *not* your mother," Mother often said.

"It—it will all be so complicated," Elspeth had said, about the lunch party, stumbling over the words, "I—I wanted it simple, quiet and—kind of—usual, Mother." She picked up Roderick and held him tightly to give herself courage while Mother tapped with a pencil on the blotter. "Don't you understand, Mother?"

"No," said Mother.

"I thought—if I could leave, just simply, as if it were every-day . . . "

"You *cannot* pretend," said Mother, "that this kind of thing is everyday."

That had stopped Elspeth, and she could not bear to have this same scene again; instead she had said desperately, "Think of the washing-up. Father and I shall have to leave at half-past two. I shan't be here to help Marlowe."

"We shall have to get used to that," Mother's voice had been cold. "I shall get Mrs. Paget from the village," and she had picked up her pen. "It will be easiest for everybody. If you thought at all, Elspeth, you would know what these last few hours will be like for us, for your father and me, though I must say Father doesn't seem to feel it; *if* you thought, but of course you don't think; if you did, you couldn't do this."

"Oh, *Mother!*" Elspeth had pleaded once again but Mother held up her hand for silence, that thin white peremptory hand that looked fragile and was strong—strong as iron. Elspeth knew how strong it was and her nerves tingled. It was almost time to go but she had not gone yet; she could still be stopped. The hand was heavy with rings; Mother always wore her rings; diamonds, rubies, sapphires. Her hand must be strong to bear those rings, thought Elspeth, and she wondered idly what she herself would have done with them when, as Mother had often said they should, they came to her. Now they won't, Elspeth had thought, with relief. No rings, no Lady Banner-man's emeralds, none of the family silver and pictures and china. Daphne will have them all. I—I have escaped, thought Elspeth, and her face glowed; she was filled with this inner contentment, this feeling of rightness that was hers now by right—or almost hers—as if it had been given to me, thought Elspeth, and she thought, it is my gift from God, my jewels and money, my family.

Mother had returned to the subject of the luncheon party. "It will be best," she said, "no matter what I feel—and it doesn't matter what I feel—be quiet, Elspeth. I won't have people saying we're bundling you off. They might think there was something wrong, a family rift, or that there was an unhappy love affair."

"Couldn't they think it was choice?" asked Elspeth. At that, Mother had bowed her head and her neck stiffened as it did when she was mortally displeased; she pulled her chair into the writing table and began to write the notes, but her hand trembled on the paper and Elspeth, watching, was smitten. Once again she had hurt Mother—for—for nothing, thought Elspeth. When I'm so happy why can't I be generous? Why must I always do it? she thought in despair; do what Sister Monica so often said she must not, seek her own way? Trying to impose her own will, instead of accepting? "In these last few days try to do, to be, everything your parents want," Sister Monica had said. "Show them how you love them . . . " and I can't be five minutes with Mother before we begin . . . No wonder they wonder at me, thought Elspeth. This rebellious and unpleasant girl to make a nun!

She had looked helplessly across the room at Aunt Bevis who had been sewing in the window, and Aunt Bevis had looked back at her and smiled. Never, thought Elspeth, had anyone as clear eyes as Aunt Bevis; they were set a little tilted as if, for all her quietness, Aunt Bevis had an extra private and particular view of the world. Is that what makes her so—large?

thought Elspeth now, so without walls? She can see over the wall—but then Mother had caught the look and asked sharply, "Bevis, where's the list? You took it when you went to the telephone. Now it's *lost*."

"It's under the blotter on the right-hand side," said Aunt Bevis. "Thursday, 2nd April, at a quarter to one," Mother had written in her clear, pointed hand. On Thursday, 2nd April, today, thought Elspeth in bed, she, Elspeth Catherine Mary Erskine, was to enter the Order of the Sisters of Mary at their Convent of St. Faith at Chiswick, where she had already spent two retreats. She was very happy about it; very shy, but no one seemed to grasp that she was either of these things.

"What are you going to be called?" her cousin Morna had asked.

"Reverend Mother has agreed that I shall be Catherine Mary," said Elspeth. "They are saints' names as well as my own."

"Sister Catherine Mary." Morna tried it, and relapsed into helpless giggles.

"Shut up, Morna!" said her sister Jean, but Morna could not shut up. Soon Jean and then Elspeth herself were giggling too, as they had always giggled all their short lives when they were together.

"Really! You girls are too silly," Aunt Euphrosyne always said, but the silliness broke out as soon as they met, though Morna was twenty to Elspeth's and Jean's nineteen.

"But a nun *isn't* funny," Elspeth had protested, shaking helplessly.

"Of c-course not," said Jean, "It's just—you—one of us—as a n-nun!"

The giggling had been all right, it was silly but easy; it was the questions, the—feeling against her—that Elspeth could not face. I wish I belonged to another family—she thought that often in these days—one of those families, in Ireland or America, where it's part of family life for a daughter or a sister or a cousin to enter an Order. In ours you would think no one in the world had ever joined an Order before. "They make it seem so extraordinary," she said bitterly to Sister Monica, who was Mistress of the Novices. "If only I could *tell* them, Sister. If only I could explain."

"Wait," said Sister Monica. "Wait and they will see."

For a long time now people had been exhorting Elspeth to wait. "Sixteen is too young. Don't be ridiculous." "Seventeen's too young." Elspeth had retorted with St. Thérèse of Lisieux, as young girls wanting to marry have retorted with Juliet. "St. Thérèse was a case apart," she was told, "Wait," and, "Eighteen is too young. Wait."

She had, of course, needed her parents' consent, and at one time it seemed that Mother, and Father led on by Mother, never would consent. Then at long last there was hope, but she still had to wait. "If, at the end of a year you still want it . . . "

"I shall still want it," said Elspeth.

"You always were obstinate," said Mother. "Even as a little thing you would rather be sent to bed or shut up in the cloak-room than give in."

The trouble is, thought Elspeth, that I have always given in—except over this. Now I can't. She did not understand how she managed to be so steady, but when the year was up, they had given their consent—if Mother's could be called a consent. Even when it was decided, Mother never left Elspeth alone. "Robert killed, Daphne gone, one might think you would realize that you are all we have left."

"But Mother, you didn't mind when Daphne went away to be married. Hong Kong is the other side of the world!"

"That was *quite* different," said Mother. "Marriage is a woman's destiny."

"But Mother . . . "

"I hope I should never be so selfish as to stand between my child and *that*," said Mother.

"But Mother . . . "

"If only I could have seen you happily married," said Mother.

"But Mother, there are other . . . "

"Husband, home, children," said Mother.

"Mother, if I were marrying a king or a prince . . . !"

It was of no use. Mother would not listen and if she had, Elspeth could not have explained.

The news had burst suddenly on the family and the family friends. Usually, over any happening or idea, Mother took Aunt Euphrosyne and most of the neighbourhood into her strict confidence—how often had Robert and Daphne and Elspeth writhed when their most private doings and feelings were made discreetly and unfailingly public. Now, until the ultimate decision was taken, Mother had not breathed a word. I suppose she thought it would spoil my chances, thought Elspeth. Young men would shy off me if they knew. I mightn't get all my dances! Now young men, dances, chances, did not matter. The news was out and everyone seemed bewildered.

"But how did it happen?" asked Mr. Baldock.

"It began when she went on that wretched French family exchange holiday," said Mother. "The daughter . . . "

Yes, there, with Jeanne Marie, thought Elspeth. Dear, dear Jeanne Marie.

"In Paris. That's where she got the idea," Mother complained.

"What a place to go to and get the idea of being a nun," said Mr. Baldock.

Mr. Baldock, a mild little man who grew violets, was Elspeth's godfather and now he looked at her as if he had been given a little seedling to cherish and it had suddenly grown into a rampant vine. "Can't *you* get this nonsense out of her head?" Elspeth had heard him ask Aunt Bevis.

"Is nonsense the right word?" asked Aunt Bevis.

"Well, no," said Mr. Baldock. "But Elspeth! Our pretty little girl!"

"She's not a little girl," said Aunt Bevis.

"It seems so unnatural," said Mr. Baldock. "Elspeth dear, are you sure?"

The family were more definite.

"She's out of her mind!" said Uncle Arthur.

"Girls get like this," said Aunt Euphrosyne. "It's usually anaemia."

"Elspeth is not the *least* anaemic," said Mother, "she has a lovely colour," and she began to cry. "She's serious, Euphy."

"I can't believe it," said Aunt Euphrosyne. "Elspeth! Not *Elspeth*! Why, she was always the naughty, disobedient one."

"Euphrosyne is glad, of course," said Mother afterwards. "She was always jealous because you were by far the prettiest."

"Mother, don't, don't say things like that!"

"It's true. At least you'll be out of the way," said Mother

vindictively. "I expect she thinks that now Larry will marry Jean."

There had been something a little sadistic about the cousins.

"They give you all the worst things to do when you're a novice," said Morna. "You scrub floors and clean lavatories and shovel coal. You do all the rough work."

"And you won't like that," said Aunt Euphrosyne. "You were always what Nanny calls backwards in coming forward to help."

"Was I?" asked Elspeth. She did not really, fairly, think she was.

"Last time you stayed with us," said Morna, "you left your towel on the bathroom floor and the tiles were all over powder and you never even turned down your bed."

"They bully you and humiliate you to find out what you're made of. I have read about it," said Jean, and she added, "If you like one thing more than another, it's taken away."

"Life does that to you as well," said Aunt Bevis. "As you will find out."

Elspeth had looked at Aunt Bevis in surprise. Aunt Bevis's cheeks had been quite pink.

The whole neighbourhood was roused.

"A well-plucked girl like that!" said Major Fitzgerald. "You should have seen the way she rode that mare of mine in the Dunbar Hunt Cup, not anyone's ride, I can tell you."

Colin Crump had blinked at Elspeth from behind his glasses and something seemed to boil up in him as if he wanted to speak; of course, no one counted Colin Crump, but there was trouble with Larry.

"I thought you were going to marry Larry," said Lady Bannerman in her gruff voice, and she said, as Elspeth thought she would, "I meant to give you my emeralds."

Elspeth was touched and went to kiss her but Lady Bannerman held her off. "Don't kiss me," she said; there was a harshness in her voice that smote Elspeth. "You hurt Larry," said Lady Bannerman, her lips trembling. "You led him on, you little—vixen!"

"I didn't." Elspeth had said that before she could stop herself. "Don't answer. Be quiet. Submit," said Sister Monica, but Elspeth was cut. Led Larry on! She might have said, "He was there before I led him," but that would have been to hurt him more. She had picked up Roderick and hid her face against him and immediately all thought of Larry was wiped away. Soon, soon, Elspeth had thought, I shall have to say good-bye to you, Roddy. Roddy's small black spaniel body was warm, silky, firm in her arms. He licked her neck and his eyes, between his absurd down-hanging ears, looked into her face. Her own eyes swam in sudden tears. She dared not keep Roderick in her arms; hastily she put him down.

"You're not listening to me," Lady Bannerman had said. "Hard as nails. You young things don't care how you hurt."

They all said that but, willy-nilly, thought Elspeth, she had to put on this front of hardness with them, or give way completely. "She has grown so hard," they said.

"Father is twelve years older than I," said Mother. "When he goes, I shall be left alone. If I get ill . . . "

"Mother, why should you get ill? You're awfully strong."

"You're like marble," said Mother, "like marble."

I'm not. I'm not. If only I were! thought Elspeth, and she had thought of Jeanne Marie who was already professed and of Jeanne Marie's father and mother and brother who were so glad. Elspeth had borrowed the old Rover from Father and went over to Chiswick to find Sister Monica. "Sister, ought I to give it all up?"

"You must ask yourself that," said Sister Monica. All the Sisters were the same; when you asked them, implored them, knelt to them, they put you gently back on your own feet.

Elspeth had looked up at Sister Monica's calm face. Sister Monica was sorting beans into bags for the kindergarten school; the infants used them for counting and Elspeth watched her fingers, picking the beans up in twenties, never making a mistake and slipping them into bags and tying the strings with a firm knot.

"Sister, help me," said Elspeth.

"Dear child, I can't help you," but perhaps Sister Monica had spoken to Mother Dorothea because the Reverend Mother had sent for Elspeth.

"If you have the least doubt, Elspeth . . . "

"I haven't, Reverend Mother." There Elspeth was firm; then the firm clearness clouded. "It's not my doubts, it's theirs. They make me wonder if I'm selfish. Mother, what should I do?"

"I think you should read the Commandments," said Mother Dorothea.

"The—the Commandments?"

"Yes. They are in the right order."

Now Elspeth understood. Her firmness shone but she cried, "If only I could *explain* to them, Mother. If I could make them see. I—I'm so dumb!"

Reverend Mother was silent for a few moments and then she said, "Perhaps you are given no words because there is no need for words. The action speaks, Elspeth," and she asked, her face serious, "Isn't that the way of the Cross?"

"But—but mine is such a little thing," said Elspeth, slightly shocked.

"A little thing but it makes you suffer. I think you have to consent to suffer, Elspeth. If Our Lord had not consented, He would have spoiled God's plan; have you thought of that? On the Cross He did simply what was asked of Him. He did not try to improve on the work of the Master. He used no fireworks," brought out Mother Dorothea after a hesitation.

Fireworks. That was a funny word for Reverend Mother to use, Elspeth had thought. It seemed almost irreverent. She sat silent, thinking, then she said, "But . . . " and remembered it was not customary to argue with Reverend Mother.

"But what? You may speak, Elspeth."

"The sky darkened," pleaded Elspeth. "The veil was—rent."

Reverend Mother was adamant. "That was given Him," said Reverend Mother. "Sometimes things are given; it's not for us to expect or ask. No. He did not use His power." Her voice grew deep with feeling. "They taunted Him and crowned Him with thorns. They told Him to come down off the Cross and prove Himself God and how did He answer? He let them win; hung there and died." Reverend Mother's face became marvellously kind and she put her hand on Elspeth's head. "He didn't ask for vindication but suffered and died—and lived. That proved Him God."

As Elspeth drove home it had stayed in her mind; she had thought about it every day since.

The second of April remained fixed. Mother's invitations went out and were accepted, and the time went quickly till it came to the last day and Elspeth woke now to that sensation of emptiness and space, the windows and doors open and the sun streaming in. On the borderland of her sleep the birds sounded like the Convent choir where the children chirruped in an unconscious cherubic singing; she opened her eyes and looked along the sun's path that seemed to go from her bed, across the garden and the tops of the trees, across the copse where she used to play with Robert, to the woods and the far sky. The path might, she thought, have been a vision, only it was the sun; the singing might have been cherubs, only it was the birds; and suddenly feeling completely happy and rational, she sat up in bed.

Aunt Bevis came in with two cups of tea. In her old paisley dressing-gown she sat down on the bed. "Well, I must say," said Aunt Bevis, "it's refreshing to go away without packing."

In the past weeks Elspeth had given all her things away; her books in the white bookcase, the doll Mignonette she had had since she was five, and Dinah, her old rubbed velvet piccaninny; all her clothes, shoes, ornaments, treasures, had gone. The gardener's children had some of her things, the cousins some. "Would Morna like my pink net dress?" "Jean, my tennis racquet's for you. What a pity you can't get into my boots." The riding boots were new, glossy, black on their trees. Major Fitzgerald had given them to Elspeth for her birthday. "Fifty-six guineas," the Major said, mournfully.

"I couldn't warn him," said Elspeth. "Mother wouldn't let me."

As she gave away her things, her happiness mounted—until other people came in. "Mother, would you and Father mind if I gave my brushes to Marlowe? I mean—she's been with us so long and she thinks they're lovely."

"You thought them lovely once," said Mother.

"I—I do now. Of course I do. I love them but I won't need them," said Elspeth.

I won't need anything, I shall be free. That was all done. This heavenly morning she was empty of things and she lay back in bed as she thought: no more fittings and bringing things back on approval and thinking what I shall wear: and my face, with its horrible freckles, won't matter: my hair and Mother wanting it to be waved and having it cut only by Mr. Charles: and not wearing the same dress twice in the same place, and new hats and having things shortened and taken in and cleaned, and washing out gloves and handkerchiefs . . . "No, not even packing," said Elspeth aloud. The new life was breaking through the old, but for this last day it had to be an admixture; in each thing, in each thought, there was both old and new.

After Aunt Bevis had gone, Elspeth dressed. It was the last time she would put on these clothes, usual clothes; a grey skirt, grey blouse, pale pink jersey, stockings, grey shoes. They would do for the lunch party. At the Convent she would take them off and pack them in a cardboard box and give it to Sister Monica.

"What will you wear?" Morna had asked. Morna and Jean were terribly curious about every detail. The Order wore a plain black habit, "Like a rather full black dress but long," said Elspeth, "and black stockings and shoes."

"Wool stockings, flat shoes?" asked Morna.

"Yes," said Elspeth and Morna made a face. "Go on," said Morna. "Tell some more."

"We wear a white toque."

"Is that the head thing?"

"Yes. For six months I'm on probation. Then I am a novice for two years. Then I change the white veil for a black and am a Junior for three more. I'm given a black cord with a crucifix," said Elspeth.

"What will you wear at night?" asked Jean.

"A nightgown, I suppose," said Elspeth.

"Don't you know?"

"I didn't ask," said Elspeth, suddenly shy.

"She took it for granted, I expect," said Aunt Bevis and she rounded on Jean. "What do you think she will wear? A black shroud?"

Aunt Bevis had promised to take Elspeth's few remaining things and send them away with her Relief Committee box.

"You had better wait six months, Bevis," Mother had said. "She has six months in which to change her mind."

"Mother, I shan't change my mind."

"No, you won't," said Mother and she said bitingly, "What is the use of hoping when there isn't any hope?"

That was one of the times when Elspeth had timidly approached her.

"Mother, if only you could be glad!"

"Glad!" and for the first time she had said to Elspeth, "What *is* it that draws you, Elspeth? What is it you see? I wish I could understand."

Elspeth took heart and cast about for words. "It's as if instead of being blown about with life, with all the days and years," Elspeth said or tried to say, "you were rooted whole in a whole place."

"But you have a place, a good home," said Mother.

"Yes, but . . ." "There are pieces in a kaleidoscope, bits of paper and rag; you twist the glass and they are whole in a whole pattern." She might have used that symbol, or: "It's like finding yourself on a map, knowing where you are, and then you know the direction," but Elspeth could only twist her hands helplessly.

"It was that horrid little Jeanne Marie," said Mother.

"It wasn't," said Elspeth hotly. Then she tried painfully for the exact truth. "It wasn't only Jeanne Marie. She was only a little part. Why, it was always," said Elspeth with sudden light. "Why, Mother, you taught me. Think. Think of hymns," said Elspeth.

"Hymns?"

"Don't you remember how you used to play and we sang?"

"Oh, yes," said Mother, softening. "On Sunday evenings."

They both remembered those mild evenings.

"There was that one," said Elspeth, " 'Loving Shepherd of Thy Sheep.' "

Mother's eyes filled with tears. "It was Robert's favourite hymn."

"But think of what it meant," said Elspeth impatiently, "what it said. Didn't you *mean* us to take it seriously?"

Mother's eyes had flickered. Seriously, but not too seriously, Mother would have said, if she were truthful, but she could not very well say that; instead she had said bitterly, "I never thought I should have to suffer by your being good!" and Elspeth had sighed. All the scenes ended like that.

There were sausages for breakfast. The table was laid with a white cloth, blue-and-white china, silver, a bowl of primroses. The coffee bubbled gently in the Cona; there was a smell of coffee, hot milk, sausages, toast, marmalade, and apples. "What will they give you to eat in that place?" Marlowe had often asked. Marlowe was worried about that; she had wanted Elspeth to take a bottle of malt and cod-liver oil. "But I couldn't, Marlowe dear." At any rate Marlowe was determined that Elspeth should eat one last good breakfast. Morna and Jean too, often talked about the food.

"You'll have lentils," said Morna, "and fish. Ugh!"

"Bread and water on Fridays," said Jean.

"No, on Fridays you'll fast, and what about Lent?"

"Listen," said Aunt Bevis. "Have you ever seen a nun who didn't look perfectly well fed?" When they came to think about it, as a matter of fact, they had not.

Mother's breakfast tray was there. "I'll take it up," said Elspeth and Aunt Bevis did not interfere.

Mother was sitting up in bed reading her letters.

"Your breakfast, Mother."

"Why didn't you let Marlowe bring it?"

"I wanted to," said Elspeth and kissed her. Mother did not say anything sharp, and by her bed, on the table, was Elspeth's miniature Dresden cup and saucer. Elspeth had brought it to her, the last of her things. Never, thought Elspeth, had she loved people as much, as—as compassionately as when she gave away her possessions. "Mother, will you have this?" and she put the little rosy cup, with its shepherds and shepherdesses, down at Mother' side.

Mother had not answered but now she had it by her bed, and again Elspeth felt that trembling love. She bent down and kissed her mother. "Remember I—I love you just as much," she whispered.

Mother sighed. "That's some consolation." They were, in that moment, closer than they had ever been; then Mother put up her hand to Elspeth's cheek; the rings felt cold and hard.

Mother sighed again, then she said, turning over her letters, "Will they let you have your own post?"

Elspeth was startled. "I—I don't know, Mother. I never asked. I don't see why not."

"Those places are full of taboos," said Mother. "I'm not going to write letters and have them pruned by the Sister Superior."

"I suppose they know best for us, Mother." Elspeth said that tactlessly, but she was trying to convince herself. Mother flushed and said something that linked straight with what Mother Dorothea had said, though Mother would have hated to know that.

"Honouring your father and mother is a Commandment," said Mother, and she gave a harsh laugh. "But of course it's a long way down the list."

Things are made clear at last, thought Elspeth, quite and horridly clear, but she could not bear it. She said, as she had often said when she had had to go back to school, "Mother, don't. Don't. Not on my last day."

After a moment Mother said, in a normal everyday voice, "What are you going to do this morning?" and Elspeth answered, as she had answered a thousand times, "Oh, all the usual things."

But that was not quite true; after she had helped with the work, she planned to go all round the house and garden and into the copse, with Father perhaps, and take Roderick for a last scamper in the woods. That's what I want to do, thought Elspeth. I want to see the house for the last time, the old white walls, the flagged path, the lavender bushes, the slated roof brooding among the trees. I shall see it again, of course, but I shall be separated, not quite as I am now. She had meant to go all over it, inside as well as out, touch each window-sill, see it all: the gleam of silver and copper and brass, the polished mahogany, the white sheepskin rug in front of the drawing-room fire; the crystal vases of cut daffodils, the books and papers, *Punch* and the *Times* folded in the paper-rack; the worn red brocade on the seats of the chairs; the patterned stair carpet, the wallpaper in the bedrooms, the Peter Rabbit frieze in the nursery and its window bars and high fender. She had meant to go into the copse and see if the wild hyacinths, that she used to pick with Robert, were out; she had meant to walk down the wood paths with Roderick, but there was the lunch party, of course.

Elspeth dusted the drawing-room and put out extra ash trays and then helped Aunt Bevis with the flowers. Mother was even more fussy than usual about the flowers.

"What would *you* like on the table, Elspeth? It's your party." That had become true. Mysteriously it had become Elspeth's party. "Of course I would do anything for you children," Mother said, pushing back her hair and smoothing her forehead where, obviously, she had a headache, "but these days the work *is* heavy. I had thought of primroses," said Mother, returning to the flowers.

"Primroses would be lovely," but when the primroses were done, Mother remembered the pudding was white and the whole effect would be pale. "It will look hideous, quite hideous in this dark room; you must get brightly colored primulas." Elspeth picked them, orange and rust primulas, dark crimson, vivid blue and magenta, and arranged them in a great bowl.

There were the best table-mats to get out—the lace in one was creased and had to be ironed; there were finger bowls to wash; she had to go down to the village for cigarettes, though she would have liked to keep out of the village. "You go off today then, Miss Elspeth," and when Elspeth said, "Yes," they all avoided her eyes and looked embarrassed; all except the postmistress, Mrs. Cox, who was jauntily confident she would come back. The Post Office was also the village shop. Elspeth had to face Mrs. Cox. "You will soon have enough of it," she told Elspeth as she handed her the cigarettes. "We shall soon have you back." Elspeth did not argue as she did with Mother; she knew she was a nine days' wonder in the village and she hastily made her escape.

When she came in, the telephone was ringing and she went to answer it. "Hallo," said Elspeth, and the voice at the other end paused before it spoke. "Is that—you, Elspeth?" it said, uncertainly. "Could I speak to your mother?" Since they heard that Elspeth was going to be a nun, their friends seemed to doubt that she could answer the telephone; but nuns telephone, thought Elspeth in irritation; they use typewriters and vacuum cleaners and go in cars and aeroplanes. They drive cars; I have even seen a nun driving a buggy very fast; they are not medieval idiots, thought Elspeth.

Everybody's nerves were getting overtaxed. Mother went to lie down, even Aunt Bevis was cross, and Marlowe, in the kitchen, was unapproachable. I didn't mean it to be like this, thought Elspeth unhappily; she looked across the lawn, where the daffodils were bending and bobbing along the hedge by the wicket-gate that led into the copse; she could see the tops of the birch trees, the milk gleam of their stems, but time was getting short and she had to help Marlowe make the pudding. It was one of Mother's favourites, mushrooms in grass; the mushrooms were meringue shells, lined with chocolate and turned upside down on fondant stems; they stood on a base of chocolate mousse decorated with fronds of angelica grass. While Elspeth was arranging them in the pantry, her father came and stood by her. He watched while she cut the angelica grass and wearily stuck it in. "Damned flummery," said Father suddenly.

"Dad, I wanted to come with you and see what they are doing in the copse," said Elspeth miserably.

He jingled his keys and the silver in his pockets. "The heavy timber's gone," he said, "except the big beech. It took two days to get that down. I should like you to have seen it. Fine tree!" Then he added, "Better do as your mother wants."

Father never made an outcry. "Your mother's a very emotional woman," he had often said to his children. "She feels." Her feelings were so strong that no one paid much attention to his. When Robert was killed, Mother collapsed, but Father only seemed more silent, to grow a little smaller, a little balder; he began to have indigestion, but he was as quiet and gentle as before. Daphne was his favourite, but when she married Cyril, and that had meant Hong Kong, he had only been anxious about her settlement; he had had to sell some of the land, some of his first editions, and take off some of the timber as he was doing now in the copse, but he never spoke of bills or worries, except perhaps about the bullfinches that had invaded the fruit last summer; he only took more sodamints. Nowadays, thought Elspeth, he always smelled of sodamints.

When Elspeth had made her decision, he had said, "You really want to do this, Kitten?"

"Yes, Dad."

He had looked at her more seriously than she had known that he could look. "You know what it means?"

"Yes."

"The privations, Elspeth, and the—deprivations."

"Yes. Reverend Mother has explained them clearly"—Elspeth might have said, terribly clearly—"to me."

"I shall have to sell out some shares," said Father. Elspeth was smitten and he said, "Don't look worried. If you had married, you would have had to have a settlement," and he put his hand on her shoulder and said what none of them had said, "This calls for something handsome."

Elspeth, flushed and incoherent with gratitude and tears, had only been able to stammer again, "If—if I were marrying a prince or a duke . . . Oh, Dad!"

Now he stayed by her in the pantry, looking at the mushrooms and jingling his keys. "I suppose your mother wants all that," and he sighed and went away.

There was one thing that Elspeth was determined to do that morning and that was to give Roderick a good brush, leave him clean, fresh, and ordered. As soon as she had finished the mushrooms she whistled him up and took him into the cloakroom.

"From the moment you come to St. Faith's," Sister Monica had said, "you will own nothing in the world. Here we don't say 'my cell,' 'my bed'; everything belongs to the Order and is lent to you. Not even the handkerchief you use is yours, you understand?"

"Yes, Sister."

"That isn't hard," said Sister Monica. "It's surprisingly easy. You will see. It will come quite naturally."

That had been true of most things, Elspeth might almost say of everything—except Roderick.

"You will remember his water, Aunt Bevis?"

"I shall remember."

But who will take him for long walks in the woods? Who will understand him? Roderick was not anybody's dog, not like most spaniels; his moods were as dark as his coat; sometimes Elspeth would think there was a being shut up in Roderick, a captured beast, who looked out of his eyes and wrung his heart and made him disagreeable.

"He doesn't mean to be cross. He needs understanding, Aunt Bevis."

"I shall try to understand him."

"When he gets a stick and puts his paw on it, it means he only wants you to pretend to take it; he wants to bounce away with it himself, and when he growls and lies by himself, he's unhappy and then you must leave him and only show you love him very much—and remember he's an actor, Aunt Bevis. When he pretends he doesn't want his food, he wants it very much . . ."

Not even Aunt Bevis could have patience for that! If—if I had known what it was like to leave Roderick, perhaps I shouldn't have gone, thought Elspeth, but that's *disgraceful!* What, mind more about a spaniel than Father, more than Mother or Aunt Bevis! How can I? thought Elspeth; but she could. A dog cannot stand in the way of humans, it is not fitting, but, "He's so innocent, Aunt Bevis." Now, as she brushed him, Elspeth saw that it was dangerous to go near Roderick that morning; she could not trust herself and tears fell on his head and ran, shining, down his black coat, helpless, warm tears.

"Elspeth!"

She whipped round. It was Larry Bannerman. Larry arrived early. He was standing in the doorway of the cloakroom, looking at her with an expression on his face that made her turn back quickly to Roderick; even Roderick was safer than that look on Larry's face. Roderick pierced her, but she pierced Larry. Oh, how silly everything is, thought Elspeth.

"Why do you let them make you go?" said Larry. His voice was angry.

"No one's making me go. I want to go," said Elspeth.

"Then why are you crying?" said Larry.

"Don't you expect me to feel it?" said Elspeth angrily too.

They hurled these angry questions at each other.

"Do you think I'm made of stone?" cried Elspeth.

"Yes," said Larry tersely.

Stone! Marble! Hard as nails! Oh, I'm not. I'm not. She began to cry again.

Larry took one step nearer. "Elspeth. Elspeth! My little love!" His voice shook with feeling.

"Larry, *please* go away."

He came nearer. "You don't want to go."

"I do! I do!"

"It's an idea that's got hold of you."

"No, Larry! No!" said Elspeth breathlessly between the pent-up sobs that shook her. "It's—it's my life." She might have said: Don't you see, I'm fighting for my life.

"Elspeth, I love you." He stood there just above her, his eyes pleading, very much as Roderick's eyes pleaded when they looked up at her, only Larry's looked down. Elspeth did not know herself what it was in her that made her able to harden her heart, even against these two; that gave her strength to do it. "Elspeth."

She whispered, "Larry, couldn't you love Jean?"

His eyes blazed and he said, "You're not the only one who

can fix their heart on something." At that Elspeth burst into sobs, crying aloud, "Oh Larry! Go aw-a-ay!" He turned on his heel and went. Elspeth could hear his steps ringing on the tiles of the back passage and she cried helplessly, her sobs stifled against Roderick's coat.

"Elspeth! El-speth! Lady Bannerman is here, and Co-lin."

Let me run away, thought Elspeth. She felt hunted. I shall go now. Say good-bye to Roderick and leave him in the kitchen with Marlowe and get my coat and bag and get on a bus and go there by myself. I can't stand it, thought Elspeth. I can't stand any more.

There were only minutes more, not many minutes, an hour or two, before that door in Chiswick would shut on her, before the calm, the peace and sanctity would ring her round and she would be safe, attained, achieved. It was near, but it seemed far away with these minutes that lay between, these painful pricking minutes. She shut her eyes and the tears ran out under her lids. I can't stand—all the—pricks.

"Elspeth, your mother's calling you." Elspeth's eyes flew open and her chin went up. It was Larry's voice again, but mercifully he did not come in. He spoke from the passage outside, and again she heard his steps going away. She heard the front doorbell ring, Marlowe's steps in the hall; then Aunt Euphrosyne's voice shrilled with Mother's. She heard Uncle Arthur's boom and Roderick struggled to get down. He had a passion for Uncle Arthur. Elspeth put him down on the floor and he tore out. She heard Uncle Arthur's *"Hullo,* little dog!" and Mother's "Get down, Roddy. Down!" and then "Elspeth! Elspeth!"

"Just getting tidy," called Elspeth in a loud voice and began splashing her face with cold water, trying to cool her red eyes. Then she heard Mother's quick pattering steps, her high heels on the passage outside.

"Elspeth, what are you doing in there?"

"I have been brushing Roddy."

"Brushing Roddy! Everyone's here."

"I'm just coming, Mother."

"You know the men want the cloakroom for washing their hands." Mother sounded cross.

"Yes, Mother."

"Come along. It looks so rude."

Elspeth combed her hair with Father's old comb, rolled down her sleeves; she would have to leave her face and hope no one would notice. "Now for it," said Elspeth and she dug her nails into her palms. She saw Mother's slight, tall form in the grey pleated dress at the door of the drawing-room; "Tchk!" said Mother and bent down to pick a thread off the carpet. Then she went in. Elspeth heard her voice saying, "Of course, the poor child has had a great deal to do." Elspeth flinched but she had to go in. Swiftly, breathlessly, she crossed the hall and in a moment she found herself taking glasses round on a little tray, handing cigarettes in the silver box as she had a hundred times before; this—this is what I have been bred to do, thought Elspeth, but after a little while she saw that everything was different; different in the way their eyes looked at her; the contrast in their voices as they greeted her; they seemed to edge away from her, draw together against her. Am I imagining it? thought Elspeth. Then she found herself talking to Colin Crump.

Colin Crump had always been a joke to them; he had been asked to every party she could remember, usually to make the numbers even or because boys were in short supply. "What happens to him in between?" asked Jean. "Perhaps he only comes to life for parties," said Morna. As long as they could remember, he had been there: first as a little boy with eyes in owlish glasses and sticking-out teeth, who stammered, then as a large boy with even thicker glasses and a gold plate and a voice that went up and down; and latterly as this young man, Colin Crump, whose teeth were straight, whose stammer was fixed, but whose glasses were thicker than ever. His eyes looked owlish still as they glowed into Elspeth's. She and her cousins had always run away from him, tried to skip his dances, particularly Elspeth; now she could not escape. "I—I think this is splendid of you, El-Elspeth," said Colin Crump confidentially, and Elspeth was startled into looking at him. "I d-don't know how you found the c-courage to st-ick out for your own way . . ." he was saying, "but of c-course you al- ways d-did."

"Did I?" asked Elspeth uncertainly.

"That's what always made me admire you so t-t-tremen- dously," said Colin.

She had never known that Colin Crump admired her, or that he could do anything as positive as admire. She felt she should say something. "Did you?" or, "How kind of you," but she could not say that. She could only smile; the smile did not feel real, it felt like a faked simper. She thought everyone in the room was watching her; ostensibly they were talking to one another, laughing, but they never took their eyes off her; they were aware of her. How strange that, in all the familiar gathering, Colin Crump, whom she had never thought of ex- cept as a joke, should be the only one to understand her. Colin and perhaps Aunt Bevis. She began to feel hotly rebellious, as if something were rising in her under all these eyes, these looks, these thoughts that were completely out of sympathy with her. At the least little signal I shall break, thought Elspeth.

She could see through the door, across the hall to the dining-room; the table gleamed with its silver, lace, and the colours of the primulas. She thought of the morning's hurry and fuss and she had a sudden vision of the refectory at St. Faith's, the empty, clean room, no curtains, only windows, the tables laid out with a bowl and cup for each Sister, who brought her own fork and knife and spoon and helped herself from a side table. She remembered the quiet eating while a young novice, perhaps herself soon, stood and read aloud. She saw the colours of the flowers under the statue of the Virgin; the flowers came in their seasons for Her, those that grew in the Convent garden; they did not have to match the pudding. That's not fair of me, thought Elspeth, then she cried: But there one isn't interfered with, broken up; there one can remember, be whole, be the whole of yourself because you are allowed to lose yourself. A longing swept over Elspeth; she felt she could not wait.

The guests had fallen into three circles. The young ones were in the window—except Larry, who kept by his mother, tossing down drink after drink. Lady Bannerman was silent but her eyes kept looking from Elspeth to Jean and back to Elspeth. Jean was looking pretty in her new tweed suit. "Is it tomato colour?" asked Elspeth.

"They call it spring red," said Jean.

"It's bright tomato," said Elspeth derisively and then remembered Sister Monica and said, "It suits you." Jean did not hear her. All of them were listening to their elders.

The men were by the fire, talking jerkily. "That damned bullfinch," said Father.

"There's a spring trap on the market now," said Uncle Arthur.

"Herring nets,"—that was Major Fitzgerald. "They will have every plum if you don't stop 'em; darned little robbers," and they began to talk about apples—a glut of cider apples—and of Major Fitzgerald's Worcester Permains. That was harmless, but on the sofa there was the sound of whispers. In spite of the forbidding silence of Larry and his mother, the women were on the topic of Elspeth. It was Aunt Euphrosyne who whispered. Mrs. Baldock leant forward to hear; her blue straw with the white bow met Aunt Euphrosyne's feathers; Mother's head was in between. "Utterly, utterly, selfish," Elspeth heard; and Jean heard and Morna and Larry and Colin Crump, the whole room, and Elspeth felt a burning colour flood her neck.

"Ribston Pippins," said Father loudly.

"Can't beat 'em," said Major Fitzgerald.

After all it was Aunt Bevis who precipitated it. Aunt Bevis had been sitting with an expression on her face that showed, Elspeth thought, that she was worrying over the food. She had argued with Mother that there was not enough chicken; "We should have had three from the farm, not two," said Aunt Bevis; now, suddenly, she spoke; perhaps if she had not been worrying over the chicken she would not have spoken as bluntly. "How dare you badger the child," said Aunt Bevis, "Yes, how dare you!" Elspeth began to tremble and Colin turned. To her horror Colin joined in. "You—you shouldn't," said Colin Crump, stuttering and swallowing. "D-do you remember," he said, and the words seemed to swell with the difficulty he had to get them out—as words are difficult for me, thought Elspeth, wishing he would be silent, but he was determined to go on. "Do you re-member, Mrs. Ersk-kine, when they c-came to C-Christ and said His mother and His brethren were st-standing without . . . ?" He could not go on, he was as scarlet as Elspeth, but, "Yes," said Aunt Bevis furiously and loudly. "Do you remember what Christ said?"

"I remember, Bevis," said Mother, her voice high. "I remember and I have always thought it was heartless. Heartless!"

There was such a silence that if Roderick had shed one hair on the carpet it would have been heard. Every eye in the room, whether it looked at her or not, was turned on Elspeth. She had never felt as exposed. Sister Monica had told her not to speak but now it was as if, willy-nilly, through Colin and Aunt Bevis she had spoken, as if she had been given a voice. Then justify it, thought Elspeth in agony.

St. Elizabeth found her apron full of roses. St. Teresa had levitation. The wind changed for St. Joan. "O God!" prayed Elspeth, her lips silent, her hands sticky.

If, through the open window, a wind had swept in and filled all the room with sound; if she, Elspeth, could have been lifted up, even two feet from the carpet, lifted without a hand touching her; if roses had fallen or their scent perfumed the room, even one or two roses, but she was left. There was no help, no vindication.

She had to stand there before them all, helpless and silent. She could feel her heart beating hurtfully; for a moment she could only feel the hurt, the smart, and then it became a tiny echo, echoing down two thousand years—no, nineteen hundred and sixty, thought Elspeth. The drawing-room seemed to swim round her and she heard Reverend Mother Dorothea's words; those near voices faded and Mother Dorothea's, calm, authoritative, directed her, "No fireworks."

Elspeth's hands unclenched, and as if she had broken the tension, everyone relaxed. The clock ticked, Uncle Arthur cleared his throat, Roderick stretched and sighed blissfully at Uncle Arthur's feet; Mother gave a quick little sob and dabbed her eyes. Everywhere conversation broke out.

"Ribston Pippins? Yes, nothing to beat them," said Mr. Baldock.

"They had a nice brown corduroy skirt with a little checked coat, but I chose this," said Jean.

"Have you heard the S-Simmonses are having a band for their d-dance?" asked Colin Crump of Morna.

"From the Crane Club. It will cost a fortune; quite ridiculous!" called Aunt Euphrosyne.

Lady Bannerman passed her drink to Larry. Larry drank it.

"Bevis, it's a quarter past. Don't you think . . . ?" said Mother, but just then Marlowe sounded the gong.

You Need to Go Upstairs

❧

After my novel *Black Narcissus,* published in 1939, had made something of an impact in America, I was inundated with the usual letters asking for gifts and donations for charities, some public, some private and, at times, very peculiar. These demands are distressing for an author, especially one unaccustomed to much money, and therefore inclined to regard as a windfall what is very much an earning. Windfalls, I felt, should be shared; fortunately I had a prudent father and a firm bank manager, and two small daughters to educate, so that most of the appeals had to go unanswered. There was one though that I could not get out of my mind—an appeal from nuns who ran a home for blind children; they did not, they said, ask for money but would I write a short story for the magazine they sent out all over America?

To write a story for someone or some cause is, of course, giving away money; few people realize that, but I wanted to help and so I wrote the little story of the child Ally.

What, I asked myself, does it feel like to be blind, especially when you are small and in any case have much

to learn? What can it be like, never to know colours,
always to be in darkness? It is a terrible thought. For days
I tried to imagine it and my family had the strange sight
of Rumer going about the house with her eyes tight shut
—but that was not enough; I had to get down to Ally's
size.

The story, though so simple, took quite a while to write
and when at last it was ready and sent, the nuns returned
it as "unsuitable"—*nice* blind children, it seems, do not
go to the lavatory! Fortunately my American agent saw it
and immediately sold it to *Harper's;* since when it has
been reprinted several times and in different languages.
The late Richard Massingham had the idea of making it
into a short film with natural background sounds; it
would have been wonderful.

You Need to Go Upstairs

❦   ❦   ❦

And just when everything is comfortably settled you need to go upstairs.

You are sitting in the garden for the first time this year, sitting on a cushion on the grass by Mother. The feel of the grass is good; when you press it down and lift your hand the blades spring up again at once as strong as ever; they will not be kept lying down.

You sit with your legs straight in front of you; they have come out from their winter stockings and are very thin and knobbly, but the sun is beginning to warm them gently as if it were glad to see them again.

Your back is against Mother's chair and occasionally she puts her finger between your collar and your skin, to feel if you are warm; you are warm and you pick up your knitting because you can knit; with your finger you follow the wool along the big wooden pins and you say, "Knit one—knit another"; with the slow puffs of wind. The wind brings the garden scents and the sounds to you; sounds of birds and neighbours and the street.

"I like it, Mother."

"So do I."

Then Doreen, who comes in the afternoons to help, brings out a visitor; voices and footsteps; Mother has to get up but you hang your head and go on knitting. Voices creaking and rustling and a sigh. The visitor has sat down. Presently she whispers to Mother, "What is her name?"

"Her name is Alice," says Mother loudly and clearly to blot out the whisper. "We call her Ally. Ally, stand up and say how do you do."

"Ah, don't!" says the visitor and you do not stand up; you press the grass down flat with your hand. It is then that you know you need to go upstairs. The cloakroom is out of order; you have to go upstairs.

The visitor's voice falls from high up, almost into your lap, cutting off the wind and the birds, cutting off Mother, so that you have to stand up.

"Yes, Ally?"

"Mother, I need to go upstairs," and you hurry to say, "I can go by myself, Mother."

Mother is looking at your face—you cannot look yourself, yet you can always feel Mother's look; now she is doubtful, but she is proud, and after a moment she says, "Very well, dear." You understand what she does not say, *"Be careful! Be careful!"*

"Alone?" breathes the visitor, and prickles seem to rise up all over you. You have said you will do it alone, and you will. You turn your back on the visitor.

From the chairs to the poplars is easy; you can hear them straining and moving their branches just enough to tell you where they are. There are two, and when you are up to them, you separate your hands the distance apart you think they will be and you do not hit them, you find them; their trunks are under your hands and you stay to feel those trunks; they are rough and smooth together; they are like people, they are alive.

On the other side of the trees is a smell of cinders where, last winter, ashes were thrown down on the snow. The smell warns you. Move your feet along the grass, don't lift them, because the path is there and it has a little brick-edge hidden in the grass. You fell over it last summer; suddenly you were down on the grass and you have a fright about falling. You won't fall, the cinder smell has warned you. You find the path. Lift your feet—one—two. The cinders are crunching, now you can go along the path to where the flowers are.

"It's wonderful," says the visitor and her voice sounds like tears. "Her . . . little blue . . . jacket."

"It's a nice jacket, isn't it?" says Mother. "We got it at Pollards' bargain counter. Ally feels it's warm and gay."

That visitor there would be surprised if you picked the flowers, one by one, and took them to her and told her what they were. "I see no reason why you should not know your flowers," Mother has often told you. "Flowers have shapes and smells as well as colours." This is the hyacinth bed; hyacinths are easy, strong in scent and shaped like little pagodas—"Remember, I told you about pagodas"—and these are crocuses and these are aconites—but Mother is not close and you remember that Schiff may be out on the path.

Schiff! You stop. Schiff is so small that you might easily step on him, but Schiff is large enough for you to fall over. Mother . . . but you must not call, you must go on. You think of falling, you can't help thinking of falling—down—into nothing until you get hit. Mother! Schiff! Mother! But you have not called and Mother is saying in what seems an ordinary voice to the visitor, but is her special loud voice for you. "How strange! With all this sun, our tortoise has not come out on the path today."

At the end of the path are two orange bushes with bitter-smelling leaves; they are bad little bushes, with twigs that catch on your coat; you don't like them and you think you will hurry past. There are two bushes in two tubs, and there are four steps; you can remember that, twice two are four. One—two—three—four, and your foot is on the last step, but you catch at the air, catch at the door with a sharp pain ringing in your shin, catch your breath and catch the door and save yourself.

Someone, somebody, has left the scraper on the step. It has been pulled right out. You stand there shaking, boiling with anger, the pain hurting in your leg, but there is no sound from the garden; the visitor has not seen.

Now you are in the house. At first it is always curiously still; and then always out of the stillness you find it. This is the hall and in it are the smells and sounds of all the rooms: furniture cream and hot pipes: carpet and dried roses from the drawing-room, tobacco and a little of pickles from the dining-room: mint and hot cake from the kitchen, and down the stairs comes soap from the bathroom. The loo is up, next door to the bathroom—it has a piece of pine-smelling brick in a wire holder on the wall.

With the smells come the house sounds, all so familiar: Doreen's footsteps in the kitchen: a whirring like insects from the refrigerator and the clocks: a curtain flapping in the wind and a tapping, a tiny rustle from the canary. You know all these things better than anyone else.

Now you let go of the door—like this—and you go across the hall. Of course you could have gone round by the wall to the stairs, feeling around the hat rack and chest, but you would not do that any more than you would go up the stairs on your hands and knees. No, you go across—like this—like this —and the big round knob at the bottom of the stair is in your hands. Dear knob. You put your cheek against the wood; it is smooth and firm. Now you can go upstairs.

You are not at all afraid of the stairs. Why? Because Mother has put signals there for you, under the rail where no one can find them, and they guide you all the way up; now your legs go up the stairs as quickly as notes up a piano—almost. At the top is a small wooden heart for you to feel with your fingers; when you reach it, it is like a message and your own heart gets steady. It was not quite steady up the stairs.

"Ally, always, always be careful of the landing." Mother has said that so many times. The landing feels the same to you as the hall but it isn't. Once you dropped a ball over, and the sound came from far away down; if you tripped on the landing you might drop like the ball.

Now? Or not now? Are you facing the right way? That is an old fright. Did you turn round without noticing? You feel the stairs behind you with your foot and they are still there but now you are afraid to let go in case you can't step away. It is steep—steep behind you. Suppose you don't move away? Suppose you hit something—like the chair—and pitch down backwards? Little stickers come out along your back and neck; the back of your neck is cold, your fingers are sticky too, holding the heart signal. Suddenly you can't move away from the stairs. Mother. Mother, but you bite your lips. You must not call out.

Through the window you hear voices—voices from the path.

Drops of water burst out on your neck and under your hair, and you leave the rail and step out on to the carpet and walk very boldly towards the verbena and warm towelling and the hot-metal-from-the-bath-taps smell.

"Is she all right? Is she?"

"Ally, are you managing?" calls Mother.

"Perfectly," you answer, and you shut the loo door.

❧

L'Élégance

I always say I will never travel in August, but books have
their seasons and the long-ago story of my novel *The
Greengage Summer* had happened in a hot August, the
height of the summer school holidays: I was fourteen;
Jon, my eldest sister, Joss of the book, had just had her
sixteenth birthday.

Though much of it is true, the story has a mask of
fiction, but to try and capture the feeling of that holiday
we, my husband and I, were forced to travel in August; I
needed to go back to the month and the place where it
was unfolded; to a small French town near the battlefields
of the 1914–18 war. We had dreaded the journey, but
as soon as we left the main routes to the south and the
sea, and drove into the green and quiet of the Marne
countryside, we found it comparatively empty—or empty
for August.

The Marne was peaceful, with its usual traffic of
barges, a few extra—and weekday—fishermen, and at
weekends, fishing clubs; the cool green reaches of
Compiègne were almost undisturbed, even the famous
Route Champagne was not busy; it was the sea, the
beaches, lidos and casinos that called holiday-makers,

but the emptiness brought a penalty; there were few hotels off the main routes and suitable for the quiet we needed.

We tried a small one called the Moderne, starred for food: the food was excellent; I remember especially the stuffed tomato and the patron's *coq au vin;* there was an habitué called Hippolyte who loved to kiss his fingers when we ordered a bottle of wine—we saw quite a lot of Hippolyte—but the beds were too short for my husband, and though there was plumbing of a kind in the bathroom, it seeped through a hosepipe connected to a kitchen tap and never yielded more than an inch of dirty water; worse, among all the pitch-pine rickety furniture there was not a spare table—the only ones were in perpetual use in the restaurant. I did not mind being dirty for a while, but I had to write.

We tried a holiday hotel ideally set among the buttercups in a meadow beside the river, but fortunately we had luncheon there before settling into our room. The moment the gong went, the dining-room was invaded, exactly as in the film *Monsieur Hulot's Holiday,* and was crammed with French holiday-makers, all gabbling and gobbling while their children stuffed or squabbled or broke into wails. The food was execrable and at the end the *patronne,* a formidable-looking lady with enormous hips, walked from table to table, asking if we had *"bien mangé,"* meaning, "You praise, or else . . ." For us it was "else"; we left.

This was the champagne country, at that season green and gold, the vineyards stretching for miles; there were cherry orchards because this was cherry country too, where the famous cherry liqueur chocolates were made.

When the champagne buyers came after the vintage, the important ones probably stayed in the guest houses of the great champagne firms, Pommery at Rheims, Krüg, Moët et Chandon at Épernay, whose exquisite Château de Saran was designed, it is said, in payment of a debt for the architect's favourite wine. We had been asked to stay at Saran, but, for the book, I needed to be not a privileged guest but an ordinary tourist among the droves who came every day to see the famous "caves"; also I did not want to be entertained, however kindly. I wanted to write.

At last we found an hotel on the banks of the Marne. It was in the country, though there was a sleepy little town half a mile away. The house had been a château and had grace and dignity: there were the balconies overlooking the garden and river, the gravelled courtyard with the blue-and-white umbrellas, the peaceful towpath walk, all described in "L'Élégance," though the name Pierrefonds really belongs to the enchanting little village and castle several miles away.

As we stayed on, hot day after hot day, I began to notice an exceedingly plain and freckled little woman who was also staying there: she was English from the way she said "good morning," but that was all I ever heard her say; she kept herself to herself in a prim way, gave her orders to the waiter in a whisper, and kept an exceedingly dainty finger in the air as she ate, a finger that got higher and higher if my husband looked at her— I don't know how she held her knife and fork firmly enough to eat, yet she betrayed herself in the vigorous way she stirred her tea or *citron pressé*—the hotel served *"le* five-o'clock" every afternoon in the courtyard.

The hotel had, too, a noisy chef who lent a rollicking air to the whole place; he was a superb cook but his voice was a roar and he stank so of stale red wine that his *bonhomie* was embarrassing.

One evening I was alone in the lounge, except for the small lady; it was then that I heard the loud "phizzt" and over my book, watched her get up and go, a step at a time, like a hen mesmerized by a powerful fox, step by step to the service door. The chef put out an arm and drew her through.

I have no idea why she went, no idea what the small scene really meant—but it gave me an idea.

L'Élégance

❦   ❦   ❦

"It's so queer not to tell," said Madeleine. "Everyone says where they are going for their summer holidays."

It was tossed into the air for Miss Mountfort to pick up—if she chose. Miss Mountfort did not choose, but went on winding the wide satin ribbon on to its card. The ribbon was fuchsia coloured, Swiss, with a central stripe of grey embroidered with black and silver. "But *wickedly expensive!*" the client had said, fingering it wistfully. The simple Madeleine would have agreed from her heart, but Miss Mountfort was one of the best saleswomen in Pope and Ransome's and, "It is elegant, Madam," she had said austerely. "One must expect to pay for that." The client had bought the ribbon.

Elegant was a word Miss Mountfort used often. Her favourite magazine, that she lived by, was *Elegance, The Way to Gracious Living*. One of the *Elegance* maxims was: A lady never gossips about her private affairs; and now Miss Mountfort noted the measure on the ribbon card, deducted—in her head—the length she had just sold, carefully wrote in the stock figure, returned the ribbon to the drawer, all without speaking. "Everyone tells where they are going," said Madeleine again. Miss Mountfort did not answer that either.

153

Madeleine knew Miss Mountfort went to an hotel in France but in five years' prying she had not been able to find out where it was. "Why won't you tell?" she asked exasperated.

"Why do you want to know?"

"I might come with you."

Heaven forbid! But Miss Mountfort did not say it. She pressed the ribbon drawer to, very firmly, and said instead, "That would be impossible."

"Why?"

Miss Mountfort and Madeleine not only worked on the same counter, at home they lived on the same landing—in fact it was Madeleine who had found the house in Howard Road where the bed-sitting rooms were large, passably clean and comfortable, each with a gas-ring and ventilated cupboard for food. Miss Mountfort and Madeleine came to work together, and if Madeleine were not going out, went home together as well. If either had anything especial to eat or drink they shared it— "though our tastes are not the same," Miss Mountfort told everyone who knew them. She said no more than that but her pursed mouth was expressive. She and Madeleine were, Miss Mountfort supposed, friends—almost cronies, she had to admit reluctantly—but "friends" does not mean "peers" and, "There wouldn't be room in the hotel," said Miss Mountfort.

"Hasn't it chalets or camping?"

Chalets or camping! The Pierrefonds! But again she did not say it; it would have been a waste of time to try and explain to Madeleine what the Hotel Pierrefonds was.

It had been the private home of a cabinet minister. That, to Miss Mountfort, summed it up; even at the station his aura seemed to meet her. The minister had travelled up to Paris every day; "They stopped the Express for him morning and evening," Madame Voday, the manageress, had told her. Miss Mountfort had never met a French cabinet minister, but every year as she stepped off the train she remembered him with satisfaction. She saw him always with a grey top hat, a frock coat, striped morning trousers, grey spats, white linen, and a dispatch case with a golden crest; he wore a small white goatee and the slip of red ribbon in his buttonhole, the Legion of Honour. He was surrounded, of course, by railway officials; Miss Mountfort always bowed most graciously to right and left as she walked across the platform to her taxi.

The minister's exclusiveness was in the hotel still. For instance, August was not its busy time. "No, we are not for trippers," said Madame Voday. The Pierrefonds' clientele drove out from Paris at weekends to lunch or dine in quiet; a few took weekend fishing rights. In the shooting season it was full, and it was here that the agents and big customers of the champagne companies stayed, so that their wives could enjoy the garden and river walks while they did their business at the great houses at Pommery, Krüg, or Moët et Chandon—Miss Mountfort enjoyed saying those names, especially Veuve Clicquot. Of course, all summer long there were the motorists who stayed only for a night; English on their way to Italy or Switzerland, or rich touring Americans—to Miss Mountfort all Americans were rich and touring—"I have experience of them," she could say with pride.

She had had experience of several foreigners, for at Pope and Ransome's Miss Mountfort was often sent for from other departments to deal with overseas visitors. "It's an advantage speaking French," she said modestly, "and of course, having travelled, I understand currencies and the export regulations."

"You have travelled a great deal?" the customers would ask, surprised, and it was with peculiar pleasure that she could say, "I take my holiday on the Continent each year."

She had read of the Pierrefonds in a travel article in *Elegance* five years ago. The hotel was on the Marne just outside the little town that to Madeleine would have been dull. . . . "Of course. It is a connoisseur's, a vintage town," said Miss Mountfort. She did not really know if a town could be so described but it seemed to her to fit the quiet mellowness of this little place among the cherry orchards and vineyards. Had the hotel been on the coast or nearer Paris or close to the race course of Chantilly its prices would have been so high that Miss Mountfort could not have stayed there at all: as it was, she could manage one week and every year she took the same room, a third floor room, it was true, but it overlooked the garden and had a balcony. For the second week of the holidays she stayed at home. "I ask you!" cried Madeleine. "Stewing in London when you can get away!"

"I can't," said Miss Mountfort. "I can't afford another week."

"You don't have to go to such an expensive hotel."

"I like it expensive."

Madeleine had never heard of that as a reason for liking before. "But what do you *do* among all those grand people?" she said. "You must be miserably lonely."

Miss Mountfort preferred to say nothing to that.

Early on the next Sunday morning she left Victoria station for Paris. She stayed the night in Paris at a small hotel on the Left Bank, but she carefully eschewed places that would, for instance, have amused Madeleine: the raffish Deux Magots, or the book stalls on the Quais. She dined at a small restaurant

near the hotel and went to bed early. Next morning was spent
walking in the Champs Elysées and down the rue de la Paix
and Faubourg St. Honoré, studying elegance. She always allowed herself a treat by buying a handkerchief at the Maison
Blanc, paying particular attention to the manners of the saleswomen. Lunch was a cake and a cup of coffee at a *salon de
thé*. In the afternoon she crossed Paris to the Gare de l'Est,
took the three-thirty train, and in the station taxi as usual, arrived just after five at the Pierrefonds.

As soon as she saw it her heart lifted. How much she liked it!
It was not a large house but it was pretty; its white walls and
green shutters matched the chestnut trees in the gravelled
courtyard that lay between it and the road. At the back the
lawns sloped down to a private walk along the river. There
was a little boat-house, a pool with water lilies; the terrace
below the house was set with white-painted iron tables and
chairs under blue garden umbrellas; the terrace was edged
with arches of white scrolled iron, up which morning-glory
creepers climbed. Each afternoon, in supreme satisfaction,
Miss Mountfort would drink a *citron pressé* at the third table
from the left.

Her routine was established. She arrived always on the afternoon of the third Monday in August, and left on the following Monday morning. If I went on Sunday night, she thought,
they might guess I have to work. She flattered herself that she
looked a woman of means—means for a week anyhow—lei-
sured, single, but quite self-contained. She knew she looked
refined; she was lucky in being small, with small bones and
little hands and feet. She was not quite as pleased with her
figure, which was undeniably plump, "especially in places,"
teased Madeleine, which upset Miss Mountfort. "Why do you

mind? It's nice," said Madeleine. Miss Mountfort's skin was pale and covered with green-gold freckles, a green-gold that picked up the colour of her eyes, green as gooseberries behind her spectacles; her hair was mouse colour but with a soft curl that she spoilt by frizzing it and putting it under a net. Madeleine was always trying to make her wear rouge: "You need colour," Madeleine often told her, and Miss Mountfort said, just as often, "No thank you." She disapproved of Madeleine's heavy rouge and lipstick, though they set off her dark hair and great black eyes.

"But don't you *want* to be pretty?" asked Madeleine. Miss Mountfort preferred to be what Madame Voday called *"bien."*

Her blue leather suitcase, though old, was good—it had belonged to her mother; her stocking and handkerchief cases matched her rose-coloured sponge bag and her quilted rose silk dressing jacket—she had made that herself from an *Elegance* pattern. Her bedroom slippers were rose-coloured too, and it all looked perfectly presentable and well-to-do, unless the chambermaid noticed everything was the same and unused from year to year. As for clothes, Miss Mountfort patronized a second-hand shop where she bought models and she had always known how to look after them. Her gloves were French and she bought her shoes at Pope and Ransome's—"even with our discount they're too expensive," Madeleine said, but Miss Mountfort made each pair last a long time. Every year, before her holiday, she bought a cake of expensive soap.

There was, to her, an infinite satisfaction in these minuscule arrangements. Her daily plan at the Pierrefonds was apt to be minuscule too: she had her morning coffee on her balcony—or in bed if the weather were not kind. She dressed, and leaving her room neat, walked slowly into the town—

slowly to make the walk last—took more coffee at the patis-
serie in the square and walked slowly back to luncheon. In the
afternoon she had a short sleep, then sat on the balcony and
read the *Elegance* serials—the numbers saved all the year round
for this. Later, she washed her face and hands, redid her hair,
and descended to the garden where, under her particular um-
brella, she added two inches to her crocheted lace. At four
o'clock she ordered her lemon, after which she went for a walk
along the river, preferring to take several turns on the private
way rather than cross the small bridge over a dyke and walk
on the public path which was used for towing barges and
fishing, public fishing; "public" instantly condemned it in Miss
Mountfort's eyes. At five-thirty she went in, had another rest,
and an hour later dressed for dinner and came down into the
lounge. This was the time the motorists arrived and the residents came in—the interesting time, thought Miss Mountfort.
She could not have an aperitif—it would have been too much
for her finances—but she found enjoyment in watching the
other guests drink theirs. Dinner was late, too late for her comfort; she and Madeleine, when they came home from work,
had a tea-supper at half past six. Miss Mountfort would have
liked to forget that fact at the Pierrefonds, but her empty stomach rumbled rudely and loudly to remind her; often it had to
stay empty until half past eight or even nine, and it was usually ten o'clock before she returned to the lounge, ordered a
filtre, and read the papers other people had left behind in the
hotel. There was a stack of them—careless, Miss Mountfort
thought; her own copy of *Elegance* lay carefully guarded on
her knee. When the lounge emptied, as it did soon after dinner, she went up to bed.

It sometimes occurred to her that in this programme there

was a great deal of rest. Well, I go there to rest, she thought; yet every year, in her lonely room, Miss Mountfort, with a surprising stab of jealousy, could not help remembering Madeleine's tales of the holiday camp where they danced and picnicked at night. "Barbecues, moonlight excursions," Madeleine had told her. "You can't imagine what fun."

"I can imagine!" Miss Mountfort had answered in her primmest voice.

"But you do *talk* to people in that hotel of yours?" Madeleine had once asked.

"Of course," said Miss Mountfort but that was not true; speaking French at Pope and Ransome's was one thing, speaking it at the Pierrefonds was another; and though occasionally Miss Mountfort came to the rescue of a tongue-tied Englishman or American, mostly she did no more than bow, morning and evening, to the other guests.

In the dining-room hers was often the only table laid for one; she could see her loneliness reflected over and over again in the Empire mirrors that hung on the green-and-gold walls, but she saw nothing to pity in it. "Myself with napery," she might have said—*Elegance* always called it napery—"Myself with silver and glass . . . with my own half bottle of wine, with the vase that holds a single red rose—such excellent taste." As she watched herself eat she became more and more mannered and as she held her fork her little finger waved daintily in the air.

"But what will you get out of it?" asked Madeleine. Miss Mountfort could have answered, quite simply, "It." It, itself; "A Way of Gracious Living." This week would last her all the year, endow her, make her different, but, "You are getting older," Madeleine said often and Miss Mountfort knew very well that "What will you get out of it?" meant, not "What" but "Who."

Madeleine had a friend, "Which means more than a friend," said Miss Mountfort dryly. Madeleine and her Stan made no bones about how they felt; even in front of a third person—me, said Miss Mountfort—Stan would pull Madeleine down on his knee; even in the street he would put his arm round her and let his hand play on her big breasts. That had a strangely strong effect on Miss Mountfort; it filled her with anger in which tremors would shake her and give her physical heartburn. "He is drunk!" she would say furiously.

"Then I like him drunk," said Madeleine and as he rocked her she would croon, "Stan. My great big Stan! Teddybear, Stan!"

"You might at least call him Stanley," Miss Mountfort had once snapped out. Madeleine had looked at Miss Mountfort with eyes that were so honest that Miss Mountfort could not encounter them. "Why do you hate us?" asked Madeleine.

She was not always as mild. It was she who had discovered that Miss Mountfort's name was Aimée; it had been Amy but Miss Mountfort had changed it—it was ironic that it was Madeleine who had been given a French name. "Aimée and never been loved!" taunted Madeleine.

"I do not wish to be loved," said Miss Mountfort. It upheld her to add, "by anyone you are likely to know."

"But it seems a queer way to enjoy oneself," Stan himself had said, "to go off by yourself all alone."

Miss Mountfort did not answer that either. If they had only known it, she was not alone—there was one final luxury she permitted herself in this week of holiday: the luxury of Raoul.

Raoul de Malencourt. That was his name. He came down

every evening from Paris; the Express was not stopped for him because he came by car. The car was left under the chestnut trees. "What is the most expensive car?" she had once asked Stan. "A Cad—Cadillac or a Rolls," Stan had said, and sometimes Raoul had a Cadillac, sometimes a Rolls Royce. Raoul wore . . . "perfectly cut clothes," said Miss Mountfort uncertainly—she was not versed in gentlemen's clothes—but his height and leanness showed them off. Sometimes he wore a blazer, dark blue, with a crest—as on the minister's dispatch-case—embroidered on the pocket. Raoul was bronzed, his dark hair just touched with grey. He had small humorous wrinkles round his eyes when he laughed. Miss Mountfort was proud of Raoul—Madeleine, who did not read *Elegance,* could not possibly have imagined him. When he walked into the lounge he knew at once where Miss Mountfort was; as he sat down by her, his eyes . . . *devoured* her, thought Miss Mountfort, and here she had a tremor, a small delicious one, not at all like the painful upsets caused by Stan. "Did you have your rest, my darling?" "Darling" was said very low because of Paul the garçon: "Never show your feelings in public," taught *Elegance.* Raoul did not kiss her, or touch her—yet.

Madame Voday always gave them the best table in the dining-room, the small one in the window. From her lonely one Miss Mountfort could almost see her head bending to his, his to hers; their reflections seemed to be in the panes as they watched the sunset, a brilliant deep pink sunset to match the long, hot, rosy day. "What did you do all day?" "Walked and lazed. And you?" "A hundred and one things. They are not important now." They ate the menu at twelve hundred francs —Miss Mountfort, as a resident *en pension,* was only entitled to the one at eight hundred and fifty. They drank . . . a

Chambertin, thought Miss Mountfort, or *blanc-de-blanc* or pink champagne—she had never even seen pink champagne. "You spoil me, Raoul." "Nothing is too good for you." Sometimes at dinner the Pierrefonds waiters found Miss Mountfort sitting at her table with her eyes tightly shut.

When she ordered her coffee in the lounge she often almost said, *"Deux filtres, une fine."* "Only one brandy?" Madeleine would have asked, and Miss Mountfort could imagine herself explaining, "Raoul does not like me to smell of spirits" and, with another *Elegance* maxim: "A lady should eat or drink nothing that taints the breath."

Then they went upstairs to bed. . . . Here Miss Mountfort had always to break off. She had to wait until she had locked the door, burrowed under the bedclothes and turned off the light before she dared to think those hot beating thoughts. *Aimée, Aimée chérie, bein Aimée."* It was a whisper, fragrant in the dark. In the dark she could forget that the whisper was her own.

It was on the second day that Madame Voday told her, "We have a new chef, a new chef and trouble!" She sighed.

"I had noticed a difference," said Miss Mountfort.

The Pierrefonds was one of those hotels in which no trace of the ruder side of service was allowed to be seen. Cleaning was done before the guests were up; no one caught sight of as much as a vacuum cleaner in action. The bedrooms were done behind closed doors when the guests were downstairs; did anyone surprise a chambermaid making a bed, a porter with a pail, they vanished like wraiths; like wraiths they would appear at the sound of the right bell. In the dining-room the food came in as if it had fallen as manna just outside the service door; no sound or smell announced it; but this year the dining-room, even the lounge and hall were filled with an unmistakable clatter; there was also the sound of a loud voice singing. Then that is the new chef, thought Miss Mountfort, marvelling. She soon learned that he would bang open any of the doors that led from the kitchen wing and walk calmly through the lounge or hall to the bar to fetch a fresh bottle of rum or kirsch or brandy; he was accompanied by the flapping of comfortably loose slippers, and he would nod familiarly to a client as he came and went.

"He is always drunk, and on red wine!" said Madame Voday in despair.

"A bad kind of drinking, I believe," said Miss Mountfort primly.

At dinner, that second night, he burst into the dining-room wiping his hands on his trousers as he stood watching them eat, and smacking his lips, an unspeakably vulgar noise. Miss Mountfort ate on, her finger daintily raised, her eyes looking steadily into the sunset, but she wished he would go away; he disturbed her thoughts.

"*Ça va?*" His booming great voice came across her ears. It was not addressed to her, of course, but to the tables where special food had been ordered.

All the food was special—"When he cooks it," said Madame Voday. "But he is lazy!" The cuisine at the Pierrefonds had been good before but now it was outstanding.

Miss Mountfort had always pronounced that it was unladylike to care about food, perhaps as a reaction from Madeleine and Stan. They liked such vulgar food: steak and kidney pie, tripe and onions, roast beef and Yorkshire pudding, chitterlings. Miss Mountfort shuddered. "Well, what kind of food do you like?" Stan had asked her, and Miss Mountfort had answered distantly, "I like real French cooking."

Stan had looked at her in a queer kind of way. "I'm surprised you do," he said, and thoughtfully, "I've been in France myself. I wonder if you really do?"

Miss Mountfort certainly did now. She had always picked at her food but on this holiday she found herself looking forward from one meal to the next—almost greedily, she thought, distressed. She could not help it; juices she had not known she possessed had woken in her mouth.

"If Chef did not drink," said Madame Voday, "he would be in Paris or Monte Carlo." She hesitated and added, "It's not only drink"—she had lowered her voice—"You may have noticed that we have only elderly maids now. I have had to send four girls away. You remember Mauricette . . ." As Miss Mountfort listened, the kind of tremors she thought she had left behind with Stan began to shake her again.

On Wednesday evening, the third of her stay, the chef came into the dining-room with his, by now, familiar smell; he reeked of wine and—man, thought Miss Mountfort. She would not call it "sweat." Gentlemen, like Raoul, smelled of clean linen, eau de cologne, and good tobacco perhaps—she was prepared to allow tobacco, providing it were good. Her nostrils twitched, offended, and she held her napkin up to her lips.

"Well, *mes lapins,*" came the big voice. *Lapins!* That meant rabbits, and to guests! "You eat well." He surveyed them benevolently, beaming at the whole room. "You eat well." It was a statement, not a question.

A party of Americans was at the next table to Miss Mountfort and one of them—an ignorant man, she thought—found fit to raise his glass to the chef. *"Formidable!"* he called, and asked how the dish was made—it was strange what fluent French the ignorant American spoke. The chef immediately crossed the room to him.

A mastodon, not a man, thought Miss Mountfort distastefully, and indeed among the small tables it was an elephant's progress, powerful but soft-footed. To her, anything unusually large was vulgar and there was something most unhappily vulgar about the man in the blue-and-white checked cook's trousers, blue shirt with rolled-up sleeves, thick white apron, handkerchief tied round the neck, and high white cap.

The chef had twinkling eyes, a low twinkle, thought Miss Mountfort. They were fixed now on the American girls whose necklines were decidedly too low. From the back of his trousers another handkerchief hung; he pulled it out as he stood talking and there, in the dining-room, in front of them all, rubbed his hands and mopped his face, then unbuttoned his shirt and fanned his chest. The Americans only laughed. Miss Mountfort picked up her fork and began coldly to eat her fish.

The chef seemed to sense her. He stopped talking and turned himself round so that he faced her table. Miss Mountfort caught her breath and the tines of her fork sounded against her plate but she continued to eat. "I *beg* your pardon," said the chef, "I did not know Madame la Duchesse anglaise was staying in the hotel." Miss Mountfort heard a laugh and looked up quickly. He was holding his two little fingers stiffly out in imitation of hers.

She tried to look unmoved—absolutely indifferent, wished Miss Mountfort—but she felt a deep, painfully hot blush rise up her neck and stain her face. The chef must have seen it too for he dropped his hands at once and turned to go; but he was not abashed; as if he were sorry—sorry, thought Miss Mount-fort, and a choking sound rose up in her—as he went, and in front of everyone, he patted her consolingly on the shoulder. Then, as if it were a signal for her alone, he let his fingers linger for a moment on her bare neck.

Miss Mountfort could not sleep that night. Her neck, where he had touched it, burned; she burned all over. "Raoul would have knocked him down," she said, but it was strangely little comfort. How could an ephemeral Raoul knock down an actual chef? "Great bloated fat man!" she cried aloud in her agitation, "Bloated fat man!" but that made no impact at all. She tried to make herself laugh, "As the Americans do," but she could not laugh. "Treat him as a character," but he was not a character to her. He had touched her—she shuddered—how could she ever face the dining-room again?

It was a tired Miss Mountfort, with eyelids that ached, who dragged herself next morning to her coffee in the town.

The chef did not cook lunch; "not unless several visitors are in," Madame Voday had confided to Miss Mountfort in despair. "He says the boys can cook for the old hens. Of course, he did not mean you, Mademoiselle."

"He meant me," said Miss Mountfort and she tried to smile tolerantly.

"You are very magnanimous, Mademoiselle."

"Not at all. I don't let servants upset me," said Miss Mount-fort. How she wished that were true.

The chef was very lazy. He had a long siesta after lunch and before lunch too, if he could. "He would sleep all day if he could," said Madame Voday. "Drink and sleep." Miss Mountfort had seen him asleep, not only outside the kitchen but even on the bench under the chestnut trees inside the front gate.

"The front gate!" she exclaimed.

Miss Mountfort had never seen an elephant lying down but she had seen pictures of a whale washed up on a beach. Asleep on the bench the chef looked just like a whale, and though the work he was paid to do was being done by the boys, in his sleep he had an animal innocence. He slept, flushed and happy, his snores filling the whole forecourt.

When Miss Mountfort came back from the town next day he was on the bench, and making her way in from the road, she had to pass him close by; she walked on tiptoe but gravel has its effect on high heels and a pebble rolled under her foot so that she lurched suddenly. Big mammals are light sleepers and the chef awoke. He opened his eyes and stretched.

Miss Mountfort was so close that, as he looked up at her, she could catch his reek of garlic, wine, and sweat. His eyes went over her lazily, then recognition came and he laughed. "Ah! *la petite duchesse!*" he said.

She drew herself up to pass immediately towards the house but before she could move, with the agility of a fat man he had jumped up and caught her. He held her by her dress, drawing it tightly backwards so that it showed the shape of her thighs and legs. "Kiss me," said the chef.

She made a stifled small sound between a squeak and a gasp, and as she tried to get away, her feet scrabbled wildly on the gravel. He drew her steadily backwards. "Let me go!" gasped Miss Mountfort.

"When you kiss me," said the chef.

She beat at him with her sunshade but the thwacks did not

seem to hurt him. He roared with laughter. "Someone will come!" cried Miss Mountfort in agony.

"Let them come," and then she was close to him; she could feel his heat, his dampness. He reminded her of Stan. "No! No! No!" cried Miss Mountfort.

"Next time you will kiss me," said the chef and he let her go.

I shall not complain to Madame Voday: by five o'clock that afternoon Miss Mountfort had reached that decision. I shall take not the slightest notice. I shall do as I said, refuse to let a servant upset me . . . and she sat down in her chair on the balcony and firmly opened the pages of the serial, but she found she could not read it; it was a story of—of love, she thought, flinching, and she turned to "Answers to Correspondents." She always liked the correspondence columns where there were soothing questions about etiquette: "Should asparagus be eaten with the fingers or a fork?" "Are finger bowls placed to the right or the left?" But the letters this month were about deeper questions than that. " . . . You must remember, my dear," read Miss Mountfort, "in these things it is the woman who leads. Are you sure, quite sure, there was nothing in your behavior . . . " "But nothing, absolutely nothing!" cried Miss Mountfort, and perhaps for the tenth time that afternoon found she was in tears.

When half past six came, she felt so low that she knew she had been silly to miss lunch, and "Just for once, because of the shock," she said aloud, "I shall give myself an aperitif."

That was wise. The vermouth warmed and softened her, yet, mysteriously, made her take a stronger view of things.

The man was half asleep, she was able to tell herself. He did not know what he was doing. After she had finished the glass, she could smile and say, "Did you think he was making a set at you?" and it was quite calmly that, at her usual time, she was able to make her way into dinner.

"But . . . what *is* it?" asked Miss Mountfort, staring down at the dish.

The whole dining-room was staring too, had been staring all through dinner. As ill luck would have it, the room was full that evening, of people with *no* manners, Miss Mountfort thought indignantly. Yet there was something to stare at.

She had sat down at her table and had picked up the menu when she had smelled an unmistakable smell and heard a soft, powerful tread; she flinched as the waiter was pushed aside; then the menu was taken out of her hand and the silver swept off the table. "I have cooked a special little dinner for you," said the chef.

"I don't want . . . I can't afford . . . I take the menu . . . I refuse . . . " The words might have been small sizzles of fat in a pan for all the notice he took. He unfolded her napkin and put it across her knees. *"Tais-toi,"* he said gently.

To *tutoyer*—! . . . But Miss Mountfort could not speak. If she had been in the pillory it would not have been possible for her to suffer more; paying not the slightest attention to anyone else, this man, this . . . servant, stood over her and . . . What will they *think?* she thought in agony.

He was in a beaming humour, directing the waiters who brought flowers in a vase, white carnations, then a bottle of wine, then soup; after the soup there was sole with white grapes, but Miss Mountfort hardly knew what it was, she was so nearly choked with mortification. "You should pray when you drink that wine," said the chef, sniffing the glass before he gave it to her.

"Perhaps they will think I have tipped him," thought Miss Mountfort, and as he suggested, she prayed, but her prayer was: "Make them think it is because I tipped him."

She did not see the sunset. The flowers on her table smelled so strongly she felt faint. "I picked them," said the chef, "I did not let the boy pick them," and he leaned down and said softly, "Take them up to bed." Miss Mountfort had always thought it would be wonderful to be given flowers by a man— the *Elegance* heroes always gave flowers—now she was given them by a chef; the bitterness of that humiliation had made her sit upright, but there were scarlet patches on her face and neck.

Then, as a final touch, this dish had been brought, a dark-looking pancake with rashers of bacon on top; it was served with potatoes in their jackets, *"à la paysanne,"* said the chef. Proudly he showed it round. "They do them like this where I come from," he said and then, winking, "It is good for a duchess now and then to taste a little peasant food," and to her he said, "It is truly French."

"But what *is* it?"

It looked like something Madeleine might have enjoyed. "I like French cooking," Miss Mountfort had said and into her ears came Stan's thoughtful, "I wonder if you really do?"

"Eat it up," said the chef, and bite by bite, with the eyes of everyone on her, Miss Mountfort had, willy-nilly, to eat it up.

"Is it good?" asked the American, the one who spoke French.

For the first time she was on a friendly footing with the

other guests, and she had to admit that the dish was far better than it looked.

"It wasn't so difficult to eat after all?" asked the chef tenderly. The tenderness in this case was for the food, not for her.

"Now what was it?" asked the American. "I'm sure the little lady wants to know."

"It's a *sanguette,* a blood pancake."

The room grew warm with interest but Miss Mountfort faintly asked, "Blood?"

"Yes. Blood."

"I have eaten *blood?*"

"Of course you have . . . often. Eaten and enjoyed it." And seeing her face, he laughed. "It's only chicken blood. You take onions and fry them," he said to the room, "and breadcrumbs and chopped parsley and slowly the blood of a chicken. It makes a pancake. She needs blood," and he put his hand on Miss Mountfort's shoulder, "for those pale city cheeks." Miss Mountfort made, again, her queer little half-stifled noise.

"Well, I must say!" said the American, pulling a face.

"But look," said the chef, "last night you had *poulet à l'estragon.*"

"Well, yes, we did."

"You enjoyed it?"

"Very much."

"But there was blood in that chicken just the same. What is the difference?" and he asked Miss Mountfort, "What difference is there?" No answer came from any of the tables. *"Merde!"* shouted the chef. "You will not have facts." Then he looked down at Miss Mountfort and softened. "But you ate it," he said, and his voice was oddly tender. "You were a good little cannibal hen and ate it all up."

She shook off his hand, pushed back her chair, clapped her napkin over mouth, and ran out of the room.

It was not till eleven the next morning that Miss Mountfort crept out and came down. There was no one about, only Madame Voday in the office. The house was strangely quiet, quiet as it had been in other years. Then . . . has he gone? thought Miss Mountfort. Perhaps Madame Voday had dismissed him; perhaps someone had reported what had happened in the dining-room? There was a moment's wild hope, then Miss Mountfort's sense reasserted itself; Madame Voday would hardly dismiss a good chef, however troublesome, for an obscure client; Madame Voday, Miss Mountfort suspected, saw a long way through Miss Mountfort.

All the same, it was an odd silence. There was no clatter in the kitchen; there were no sudden eruptions towards the bar, nor, as the morning grew hotter and the shadows under the chestnut trees shortened, was there a whale asleep on the bench. Perhaps he has gone fishing, thought Miss Mountfort; I must avoid the river. It was time and past for her walk into the town; why then did she turn across the lawns?

The river bank was deserted, and on this golden day there were no residents in for lunch. She ate solitarily in the dining-room. The second waiter served her but hardly a word passed between them; the lunch itself was bad; the chef had obviously not even planned it. Miss Mountfort soon folded her napkin and went upstairs.

In her room she had another fit of weeping. Her nerves were completely upset. Though she had come up to rest she could not keep still.

The bedroom seemed dull and hot; she could not open a magazine; her tongue felt stiff from days of silence. The afternoon stretched long and empty. Suddenly she would have given anything to see Madeleine.

All her beloved arrangements were there; she was free, unmolested, to carry them out; no impudent servant had worried her today. Then why did she feel so flattened and, yes, dull?

What did she want? She did not know. She only knew she felt what Madeleine had said she would feel, "miserably lonely." "He made a fool of you," she told herself and it was true; she still scalded and writhed with shame and yet, persistently, she said, "He meant well and he was very drunk." Immediately the unkind question arose, "Can a drunken man mean anything?" She did not know but, "I like him drunk," she said and stopped, appalled. Those were Madeleine's words!

The afternoon dragged on as other afternoons, but none, she was sure, had ever been as long as this; it lasted—from Egypt, thought Miss Mountfort, trying to remember the farthest-away point she had learned in history. Thinking of Egypt she thought of sand, dry, arid sand, deserts. Deserts of afternoon, she thought, deserts, with a merciless glare in which she saw herself, Miss Mountfort of the careful little arrangements, the finger-in-air, she who was made sick by chicken blood, she who was called Aimée, yet had had to invent a Raoul because she had never been loved. "Tomorrow," whispered Miss Mountfort, "tomorrow I shall go home," but sometimes life does not only pierce; it hammers the nail in.

That evening in the lounge she took another aperitif. "As I'm leaving I can afford it," she said, forcing back the tears. She was sipping it when the new couple came in.

They had left their car in the courtyard, a long low car, and to take a breath of air, perhaps too from curiosity, Miss Mountfort went out and walked round it. She was afraid to leave her glass in case Paul whisked it away, and carried it with her. The car was a Bristol. She had never heard of one but she took note of the long bonnet, the white paint and dark green leather. "It's a speed car," said Paul when she went in.

The couple were English, not young, not yet middle-aged. "Thirty and thirty-six," decided Miss Mountfort. "A perfect age." She peeped over her glass at the man's height in the dark grey flannels and tweed coat; he had the bronzed skin, the dear quizzical wrinkles, the silver-grey hair, but he made Raoul seem like some film actor; no, Raoul could not compete. As for the lady . . . Miss Mountfort was suddenly heart-sick. It was for women such as this that exclusive shops like Pope and Ransome's were run and in that world she, Miss Mountfort, belonged on the other side of the counter; she had a vision of herself selling that fuchsia ribbon. "Bring me another vermouth," she said.

In the dining-room she was glad she had had that extra drink, for Madame Voday led the newcomers to the table by the window. The room was quiet and though the dinner bore every trace of the chef's presence, he did not come in. "What a relief!" said Miss Mountfort under her breath, but as she said it, she remembered the big tenderness of his voice. "I will have a bottle of—of Chambertin," she told the waiter.

"A demi, Mademoiselle?"

"A whole."

The two in the window had the menu at twelve hundred francs. They ordered *blanc-de-blanc*. "You spoil me, Peter." Had Miss Mountfort really heard that or was it because her head was beginning to swim? Peter was a far, far better name than Raoul.

"Darling." She certainly heard that. A *bouchée* crust stuck in her throat, which was sore from her crying upstairs. At the hurt, the tears began to run down her face again. She wiped them on her napkin and drank some more wine.

When Miss Mountfort got up to leave the dining-room she staggered. She heard the waiters titter. I must look very funny, she thought. I have become a figure of fun for the whole hotel, and she said aloud, "What does it matter?" Her spectacles had fallen awry. That did not matter either. She had not needed spectacles to see what she had been forced to look at all through dinner, two heads against the panes, against the rosy sunset.

She succeeded in getting herself to the lounge and sat down. "A *filtre* and a *fine*," she said.

"*Une fine*, Mademoiselle?" The waiter sounded disapproving.

"*Une fine*." Miss Mountfort rapped out.

Then the two came in. She kept behind the paper but she heard what they said.

"Pete, I'll go up to bed."

"I'll just see to the car and come up."

A pause, and then, "Come soon."

Miss Mountfort turned her head against her chair and closed her eyes. A tear ran out from under her lids. She heard the woman get up to go, pause and say "Good night." Miss Mountfort did not answer. More tears came.

"Phizzt!"

It was an unbearably rude noise but Miss Mountfort opened her eyes.

"Phizzt!"

She sat up and looked towards the service door. The chef was standing there. He was in his trousers and shirt but without his apron and handkerchief and cap. He looked curiously undressed as if . . . he were wearing pyjamas? thought Miss Mountfort. Giddily she noticed his ruffled dark head.

"Phizzt!" and he jerked his head over his shoulder. Miss Mountfort knew that gesture. It was one that Stan used when he . . . *wanted* Madeleine.

Dazed, Miss Mountfort found herself standing up and in a curiously zigzag fashion she went across the lounge. She reached the green baize door and the chef put out his hand, his great flipper; it fell on her shoulder; he pulled her to him and shut the door.

Presently Paul came and took away the unused *filtre* that had gone cold. The *fine* he drank. Then he picked up *Elegance* where it had fallen to the floor and put it on the stack of other papers that the Pierrefonds visitors had left behind.

❦

Whither the Swans and Turtles Go

❦

For part of the last war we, my two small daughters and I, ranked as an "abandoned family," the name given to families when the husband and father had gone with the army overseas. It was a difficult and sad state—especially for us because we had been abandoned in a deeper sense —but we found a refuge for a time in the out-bungalow of a Himalayan tea-garden, eighteen miles below Darjeeling.

I have written about this time in a sort of diary-journal called *Rungli-Rungliot* or *Thus Far and No Further*, which is the meaning of the Paharia words. The name was given to our bungalow because it stood on a high knoll where, legend tells, a holy Lama stopped the great flood—perhaps the same flood as Noah's. As the flood rose, threatening to engulf the whole world, the Lama continued to say his prayers; the terrified people went and interrupted him and by and by he took a moment off, came out on the knoll, stretched out his hand to the swirling waters, and said, "Thus far and no further." The water stopped and began to go down. The Lama went back to his prayers.

Rungli-Rungliot was unbelievably beautiful and

unbelievably lonely; the manager's house was four miles
away and we had no car; with all his assistants gone to
the war, he was overworked and could only pay us an
occasional visit; we saw almost no one except our few
servants and the tea-garden coolies. Life was primitive,
the war threatening, worries multiplied, yet all the time
we lived at Rungli-Rungliot we seemed to be under the
protection of the Lama's yellow hand.

The loneliness and quiet were fruitful—for me as a
woman and a writer—and for the children. We had left
Calcutta in a hurry and had brought few books or toys, so
that in play they had to use their imaginations; though
we gave a Christmas party for some of the Paharia
children, there were no child companions who spoke our
language; there was time for thinking, for wondering,
and my elder daughter, in particular, asked many, many
questions and some of them turned into this study of the
cheetal fawn. It is a study, not a story, because it is not
fiction, though I called that daughter "Hero," and turned
the younger one into a very different character, a boy.
We were sent the present of the little fawn; its memory
has haunted me ever since.

Whither the Swans and Turtles Go

❧ ❧ ❧

The inside of the cage smelled wild. That was the beginning of the moment.

The moment was even smaller than the space of the bungalow's little garden, against the Himalayan forest of the mountain, but the garden had endured for fifty years, and for Eleanor time would not engulf this moment; it would live for her as long as she lived; and it would live for Hero too.

Eleanor had been gardening when the little man came out of the forest towards her and put his burden down beside her on the grass; she remembered afterwards that the colours of the pine-tree trunks had been the exact colour of a cheetal deer's coat, excepting its spots and the flock of its tail, of course, and these were the white of the cotton-wool clouds that floated in between the trees. It was both a wild and a tame afternoon. The path came down through the forest between the trees, and the sun striking through them was brilliant with a strong reddish light.

The little man came out of the sun, unslung from his forehead the wickerwork band that had borne the hutch's weight, let the hutch drop from his back to the grass, and knelt down by Eleanor and opened its slats. From the hutch came a strong, wild scent and inside it, in the corner, was a young cheetal fawn. It was very young. "When you pick it up," said the letter, "on no account pick it up like a dog. Take its hind legs firmly in one hand and pick it up with the other or you will be severely kicked," but the fawn was folded into a cruel stiffness by the small hutch and its legs were helpless; they were thin as chop-sticks, their skin stretched like satin over the hardness of the bone; they had no flesh, no strength, and Eleanor picked the fawn up exactly like a dog, but it was wild, primal, and the helplessness was false; she knew it would kick as soon as it could.

The fawn did not like to be touched; she felt its body shrink away from her hand, and when she lifted it up, make itself hard and tense. It had suffered: a tide of suffering came out of the little horn-marked head into her hand. The head had two marks like little curls where horns would presently be. She considered its face; the upper part of the face was broad with the eyes beautifully set, peculiarly black and peculiarly shining above a black, shining nose from which the bones ran innocently and sweetly to the eyes; they told that it came from a species that had never harmed anyone, but it was not meek, it was free; even on its baby face was stamped an arrogance that was free. Now it was lost, it was not itself, it had no chance to be itself; it bleated perpetually with a wild hungry bleat, a whine that called its mother.

Eleanor called the children. Hero knelt down on the grass and took the fawn's forefoot into her hand. "Look at its hoof," she said in a whisper; "as small as a berry." She meant a goat-berry, a dropping; in smallness and blackness it was almost the same. "And it has a hoof on every foot," said Hero in a whisper.

"I want it to be mine," cried noisy Kenneth, and the fawn flinched as he shouted, "Mine. Only mine. Mine. No one else's. Mine!" But Hero was uneasy. "Why does it do—like that—and like that—and like that?"

"It wants its mother."

"Then why doesn't she come?" asked Hero, looking round the garden and into the forest.

The letter was confident: "A fawn should be fed little and often, milk and an equal quantity of water and a teaspoon of glucose—you will find it goes well. Here is a bottle." The bottle was a thick glass and the teat had a rubber smell; it was the kind of bottle a fat baby would guzzle, but to offer to a free little fawn? Even Hero was doubtful—"Will it like it?"—but Eleanor was well used to other people being more practical and wise than she, and she mixed milk, water, and glucose as she was told and brought the bottle to the fawn. She held it upright on the grass but the thin legs splayed out and tottered, and Kokil the sweeper, who looked after the animals, had to come at her call and hold it, while gently, gently she turned its head with her hand; the fawn smelled the milk, nuzzled the palm of her hand with its lips and turned and sighed and drank. It tried to be lusty and butted, the flock of tail wagged, then it dropped the teat and sighed again. "It doesn't like it," said Hero. Presently the fawn sank to its knees, turned its head back on its flank and slept.

The garden was really a clearing in the forest, and the fawn's own natural wind soughed in the trees, the deep pink of the overblown, half-wild roses dropped anywhere on the beds or on the path, or blew to the forest edge and into the forest; here dogs need not wear their collars, the Bhutia pony wandered where he wished; they were all free within the precincts of the garden fence, but Eleanor thought, what good would that be to a fawn, a young deer used to roaming for miles?

"Perhaps we can keep it till it's older and then let it go."

"It would die," said Kokil.

"Then we shall have to keep it," said Eleanor, and sighed.

"It will still die," said Kokil.

Eleanor gathered up her gloves and trowel and roots. Kokil gathered up the sleeping fawn and put it back in the hutch.

"Why do you do that?"

"It has become accustomed. It is happier there."

"But it shouldn't be. It mustn't be." The strength of Eleanor's feelings about this were suddenly so intense that she had to turn away from Kokil. Painful tears were in her eyes, but what Kokil said was true; the hutch had become the fawn's mother, its refuge, its right. Without the hutch it bleated; it clung to the cramped shelter. Though Eleanor and Kokil put the fawn down on the grass again, nothing would take it from the hutch; it crept back there, distorting its back and legs so that it might crouch there alone. It could and did wander feebly across the grass, tottering among the dogs who came to sniff at this strange new creature; the fawn was too ignorant or too young, perhaps too sick to care if they were enemies, but every minute or so it trembled back to the hutch. The hutch was of bright reddish wood, like the pine bark, like the skeleton of a cheetal doe covered with cheetal skin. Eleanor dipped her finger in honey and offered it to the fawn; it sucked and flipped the scut of its tail, then sank away and hurried, with what hurry it had, back to the hutch.

For Hero it was particularly interesting that the fawn should have appeared just now in the long autumn days when everything was momentous to her, when she seemed visibly to be growing and stretching in the length of their hours so that each day seemed as if it would go on "for ever and ever," said Hero. She knew it could not last for ever because each day had a definite shape, like the world, and she knew it was held, like the world, in a cup of pale blue sky that was not really the shape of a cup but the shape of a shell. She did not see the darkness; the evenings were late and when she woke the light was already in the valley, stretching through the pine trees close to the ground, making the undersides of the bushes gold, outlining every leaf with light. When she went to bed the dusk was coming but not the dark; at dusk most of the colour went out of the earth but it was not dark; the sky was pale in an immense dome of light and every evening a star, a single one, appeared in the dome and seemed to grow larger and larger as it went down the sky in the west. "The minute I go to sleep is the minute that star touches the earth," said Hero. "I never see it go."

Kenneth always meant to lie awake to catch that star. "I don't believe it touches," he said fiercely. "I believe it skids." They lay awake till their eyes ached, but they never saw it go.

There was a stream where they played; it gushed from a spring and settled to earthy pools and gushed away again in rapids down the mountain over stones into other earthy pools. The pools were all small and fringed with ferns, and sometimes they held fish. Hero had a pocket-sized bucket and she found she could make a pool in it too, with stones and ferns, and once she too had a fish. When they had to go in for midday dinner she was forced to empty the bucket out; a flash and a splash in the sun and all trace of her pool was gone.

Things were continually gone. Where do they go? This day
—yesterday—the pool in my bucket—where have they gone?
Kenneth had a song he sang: "Where do flies go in the winter-
time?" But this was not like that, a joke. These things were
gone for ever. More and more now Hero was beginning to
notice this, to wonder where things had gone.

Eleanor did not dare leave the fawn outside at night because of the cold and because of leopards. As soon as darkness
fell she had the hutch brought indoors and put in the small
whitewashed room that was called "the office." Hero wondered
if the fawn might be afraid of the big clock in the office.

The clock was old and confused, striking at random, con-
fusing the hours. Hero hated it because the face said one thing
and the voice another. For her it upset the march of the day.
"Crok-crok," said the clock at half past three.

"Don't you mind what the clock says?" she asked Eleanor.

"I don't notice it."

"I notice it," said Hero. She liked everything to be quite
clear and defined.

The fawn did not mind the clock. When Eleanor went in
early at five in the morning to feed it she listened by the
hutch; there was absolute stillness. When she opened the slat
and took the fawn out, it was well, curiously warm, sleepy,
and the smell from inside the close hutch was strong.

After the fawn had fed she set it outside in the early sun-
shine. It wavered and stood looking round on the drive and
put its head into the palm of her hand. Again she could feel
the two immature, premature bumps holding the promise of
horns; the bumps were confident of the future and cheered
her. She stood beside the fawn letting her hand hang down
and be pushed gently by its head.

At half past five the light lay unevenly over the valley and the top was shut in by heavy, fleecy clouds. The garden was wet and smelled of pine needles and lemons and roses. It was cold because the sunlight was still thin. She put the fawn back in the hutch and herself went back to bed.

The fawn was fed three times again in the morning. "It has some sense," said Hero. "It drinks."

Eleanor thought if she had been the fawn she would have refused. She would rather have starved. "Soon it will follow you about," the letter had said. "Be tame." That was manifestly true. Already the fawn had learned to trust her; though it knew she must torment, it seemed to know she would torment as gently as she could, but where was triumph in that tameness? She would have put the fawn back in the forest at once, but that would have been abandoning it to marauders. She remembered other tame cheetal she had seen, kept in wire-netted enclosures, the netting between them and the spaces they saw. She remembered one that was kept in a cage with birds, living under the beatings of their wings; there had been a parrot chained to its perch, wild squirrels, and a wild hare. "I had a racoon but it died," said the owner.

"It escaped," said Eleanor.

"Oh, no, it died."

Kenneth again wanted to establish rights over their new property. "We must call our fawn something," he urged. "Let's give it a name."

"If it were wild," said Eleanor, "it wouldn't have a name."

"Then how would its mother call it?" he asked in astonishment.

"She wouldn't. She would send out a feeling and the fawn would know what she meant."

"Without any words?" asked Hero.

"Without words."

They were more astonished. "Tell us some more," said Hero. Eleanor told as much as she could.

The jungle life of the fawn began to have an extraordinary fascination for Hero. She made Eleanor tell about it so often that the two lives seemed to be running parallel, the life of the jungle fawn and the life of the little fawn moving feebly on the grass of the lawn.

"Tell about the trees. What sort of trees?"

"Mostly they would be sal trees, I think."

"Are those wild trees?"

"They look wild," said Eleanor. "Their stems are patterned like a giraffe's neck and they have enormous leaves; in the dry weather the leaves turn a dark purplish colour and fall off the trees and rattle with dryness on the ground; the forest men set fire to the jungle then, and all the animals have to run before the fire. Every night the fires are lit and every day the smell of wood smoke is strong in the sun and the fallen trees are still smouldering; the trees that stand are charred to half their height and all their leaves are burnt. The jungle is desolate and dead but soon, through the black ground, the fresh green grass springs up and the deer and wild elephant come back wherever it comes."

"They come back?"

"Yes, they come back."

"Tell us some more. Tell what else is in the jungle."

"There are monkeys, nice-looking monkeys, yellow, the colour of pollen, with long white tails. When they hear anything these monkeys drop down from the trees and run away on the ground. They don't swing about from tree to tree; and cheetal, when they hear anything, canter away hardly crackling a leaf; you can see their little cloven heels lift as they jump a log and they flick their tails so that you see a twinkle of white long after the rest of them have disappeared."

"What else? What else would there be?"

"Butterflies. Always butterflies, and if you see a chain of butterflies, long like a scarf, you know there has been a kill and they are fluttering over it."

"Do wild things die?"

"You know they do. There is always death in the jungle, as there is always life."

"Must there be?"

Eleanor could only say, "There must."

"If they die they don't come back, do they?" asked Hero, and she turned to Eleanor. "Say they do."

"We don't know what they do. They are gone."

"I don't want to think of it," said Hero, and she said quickly, "I liked that about jumping the log."

In the afternoon she offered to watch the fawn. She lay flat with her elbows in the grass and felt the blades tickling against them; she liked that, each touch made her feel more alive. She watched the fawn which was out of its hutch, trembling from side to side by the rose-beds. She watched the light move over it. Light could move on a little fawn and light could move on a mountain. Little and big, they are all the same, thought Hero, biting a piece of grass. All the same. All the same, and she waved her heels gaily in the air. If she rolled over on her back she could watch the clouds drifting across the blue shell of space that held the day. When she watched the clouds she could see the world turning; it was the world that lifted slowly, with all the lands and seas and rivers and mountains and val-

leys and forests and clouds curled down on its breast; everything, their valley was curled on it and their mountain and the
river and this forest that came up to the garden and went
down to the jungle, and the jungles that joined the forest and
lay below it and went far off into the plain. Then, if the world
was so big, how could things—live things—escape from it?
Where did they go?

She sat up and watched the fawn. The sun was getting
lower, the light more rich, growing stronger and more red; the
light dappled the fawn, dappling its flanks as the necks of the
giraffes were dappled and the stems of the jungle trees. "It was
nearly this time yesterday that you came," Hero told it; and in
that time there had been a day and a night and a day. It is all
wider than it sounds, thought Hero, and she was astonished to
think that time held so much; her thoughts seemed to lead
backwards and forwards like a shuttle weaving the moments,
hours, days together into a pattern that she could not see
clearly but in which certain things seemed to be repeated or
picked up one from another: red sun and the clock croking
away the time: elephants and roses, cloven heels as black as
berries: her own heels waving in the air: the trees: the big
leaves, and the sun. Everything, every day, leading to something else.

She stood up and went to the fawn and caught it. The fawn
was easy to catch because it could not try to escape; she girdled
the small neck with her fingers and thumbs, a neck full of
muscle, hard and tough for all its slenderness. The fawn was
better, stronger altogether, than it had been yesterday. If Hero
had picked it up, probably it would have kicked.

The fawn sank, as it often did, suddenly on to its knees in
the grass; Hero knelt beside it and stroked the warm flank.

The flank was red; the spots would not show until the fawn grew older, and where the skin looked like satin it was really separated hairs, fine, reddish, all lying in the same direction; they seemed quite equal in colour and yet the tone of the little fawn's coat varied from tail to scruff: it was darker, nearly sorrel on the shoulder, and pale, fine red-gold by the scut, the same colour as the top rays of the sun high up among the pine trees.

"When you have been with us a little while you will get your spots, and then some hairs will be different," crooned Hero. "And you will forget the day you came, and this day too; now it seems long—I am surprised how long it is—but soon the days will go in like the hairs in your coat, like the minutes into this day, to a single piece, and you will forget." As she got up to cross the lawn she saw a plenitude of days, herself walking in endless afternoons, as she was walking away now with the fawn wandering after; endless afternoons but all curved with their separate arch of sky, one after the other in a scalloped pattern through which walked Hero and after her the little chestnut fawn, without a string, without a lead, following her for love; and the days grew smaller and smaller as they went away into the distance, smaller and closer together until they became like single strokes, until they were all one. "We shall keep you," said Hero. "We shan't let you go away."

Kokil came out and fed the fawn and folded it into the hutch which he carried into the office.

Hero was peeping at the fawn. "It's nearly asleep," she said. "Where would it sleep in the jungle? Tell about the night. Tell about the jungle in the night."

"In the jungle at night," said Eleanor, "it's still, with a stillness you don't hear anywhere else; it's not forest stillness because even the trees are still. There is very little wind in the jungle. A jungle cock and his hens make a sudden loud clopping noise and a loud rustling as they go through the jungle; if you were there and not used to it, you would think they were a large animal. Then perhaps a bear makes a dreadful noise stumping and clumping, and an elephant crashes and threshes at the trees. Here the stars at night seem very far away . . ."

"Except our star."

"Except our star, but in the jungle they are part of the jungle and they seem to press down through the trees and make them big. It is all so big in the jungle at night that even a forest fire looks like another star; and in a safe place in the ferns, far away so that the fires are small to it too, the mother doe makes a bed for the fawn; in ferns or in the grass, treading them down to make a tiny space." Eleanor looked sadly at the quiet hutch. "Now," she said, "it has changed all that for the clock."

"Crok! Crok! Crok!" said the clock. There was no more sound from the fawn.

That night was the first night Hero ever woke in the dark. Afterwards she remembered it, but had a feeling that she remembered it, not for what she knew about it but for something she did not know.

She woke, and it was night and still. She opened her eyes wide into the darkness. Was it jungle stillness? No. Faint and very far off she could hear the movement of the forest trees. The darkness filled her eyes, seeming to press them wider open, and as she looked into the dark she was on the fringe of something immense; more than immense, immeasurable, without measure, and she looked into it without wonder because wonder was stilled and because a spark of that immen-

sity was in her too, was herself, Hero. She knew that the
fringe of her eyelashes was a tiny thing, but still she could not
measure the power of sight in her eyes, nor what it could do
nor how long it would last; she knew only that it was there,
and through its power, coming from Hero and in Hero, she
was joined to the world that it saw, that she saw. She grew
dizzy. It was too big; the feeling of being the world was too
big; she was slowly, slowly tilting as she had seen the world tilt
that afternoon as she lay on her back in the grass. Is that
where we go? she thought, go away to become a bit of that
hugeness, to be lost in it like one of the days I was thinking of?
Like one of the hairs in the fawn's coat?

She was suddenly afraid. She felt stifled in the dark, and sat
up, then found she could see out of the window and see the
starry sky; in her bewildered mind, still thinking of the fawn,
the forest stars were forest fires and she was in the jungle.
Near to her and quite distinct she heard a sigh, and as Eleanor
had said about the junkle cock and hens, it sounded loud,
very, very loud; the back of Hero's neck went cold, but it was
only Kenneth sighing in his sleep.

It was Kenneth, but she was weak with having been so
afraid and she lifted her hand piteously; she would have lifted
her voice piteously too, when her hand felt the satin of the
eiderdown on her bed; it was a soft satin, worn and made
rough with use. She stroked it with the palm of her hand; it
was familiar and it brought her comfort. I shall play I am the
fawn and my mother has trodden me a bed in the ferns, green
ferns that meet over my head; and then she lies down beside
me and I can't see the fires, nor even the stars; if I look out of
my fern cot I can see only my mother, stroke her like this—
like this—like—this . . .

The next morning when Eleanor went to the hutch the fawn was lying on its side, and did not start and shuffle itself up as it usually did when the slat was raised. It lay still. She lifted the head and it fell limply back into her hand. She felt the heart. It was beating—just beating—almost not. She lifted the fawn out and called loudly for Kokil.

"What has happened, Kokil?"

"Make it warm. Quickly."

"It is warm."

The fawn was warm and limp. They tried to give it brandy. The drops spilled out of its lips. Eleanor tried to rub its heart and Kokil rubbed the slender thin sticks of legs. The fawn only drooped its head lower and lower until it fell across Eleanor's hand and died.

"But why should it have died?" cried Kokil. "I knew it would, but why did it?"

"You fed it yesterday," said Eleanor slowly. "What did you give it?"

"I gave milk."

"Milk? No water?"

"Milk and sugar," said Kokil, and he stared at the dead fawn. "Should I have given water? Perhaps I should have given water. It would have been better perhaps to have given water."

But could a fawn die of milk? Had it? Eleanor supposed it had.

"I wonder where the fawn went?" said Hero. All the morning she stayed close to Eleanor.

"We buried it, didn't we, silly?" said Kenneth; but Hero still hung round Eleanor.

"Where do you think it went?" asked Hero.

Eleanor had not been fond of the fawn; for her it had been more worry and pity than fondness, yet she was filled with a sense of tears unshed and a curious distaste.

"Where do you think?" asked Hero persistently.

"Whither the swans and turtles go, I suppose," said Eleanor.

"Swans and *turtles?*"

Eleanor said nothing. She scratched on the wood of her desk with her pen.

"Once," said Hero slowly, "once on a winter afternoon, do you remember, we did see swans? And they *were* going. They were going away in the sky like a thin string until we couldn't see them any more. They were wild swans and they flew away. You said they always flew away in winter, but we didn't see them again. But turtles," said Hero, "turtles are like great big tortoises. Then they go slowly, so slowly. Unless," said Hero brightening, "they swim away into the sea."

❦

Note: The "turtles" in the Marvell poem were, of course, turtle doves, but Hero took them to be water turtles that swim in the sea.—R.G.

Time Is a Stream

🌷

"Time Is a Stream" was a forerunner of what, perhaps, is my biggest novel, *China Court,* in which the house that had held five generations of Quins was an admixture of my parents' two Cornish homes and of a much larger house I used to visit in Blisland. In the short story Mrs. Quin is called Mrs. Throckmorton, but both characters have much in them of my mother.

My mother had fallen in love with Darrynane, the first home we had in Cornwall, from the moment she saw it. My father never really liked it; he believed in solid things—granite, brick, stone—and Darrynane House was ramshackle, not unlike an Indian hill bungalow: it was built on the side of a hill; parts of the road up to the village were one in five.

Year by year my father sought to prise my mother out of Darrynane; "prise" was the right word because she had set into it, taken root, deep root. She understood the villagers, and something rare among the Cornish with English outsiders, they understood and liked her. My mother had loved Indian hill bungalows and hills; she was blissfully happy. She loved the odd semibasement kitchen that seemed set in the garden; she liked the

roomy living-room where, in summer, the white
rhododendrons behind the house seemed to press up to
the window-sills, and the spare bedroom, on ground
level, that had flame and pink and orange reflections on
its walls from the azaleas. She loved every view from
every window.

She loved the garden even more than the house. It was
a rambling garden with a long drive where blue
hydrangeas—truly blue, not a pink one among them—
grew higher than our heads; the garden proper, with its
granite outcrops, was a natural rock garden where
Cornish flowers grew. A meadow led down to the woods
where beech trees stood in moss and ferns, and in the
spring, unlike other beechwoods, there were sheets of
primroses. There was a stream and a waterfall and long,
long vistas across the valley. My mother loved it all and
year after year she resisted my father.

Then, like Mrs. Throckmorton in the story, her body
turned Judas: she was found to have a troublesome heart,
odd chokings; heavy gardening was forbidden, steep
hills became impossible, and it became apparent she could
not stay in Darrynane. It was put up for sale and my
father found another house, this time after *his* heart; it
was of granite and nearer his beloved sea.

It fell to me, at that time the only daughter in
England, to help with the move and I had to witness my
mother torn away from this home she loved. It was she
who ran after the removal men, begging them not to
move the things they had come in order to move; she who
commanded them to "put that down." For a long time she
did not care what happened to her, nor where she lived.

After the long distressing day I went to my room in the
hotel where we had taken refuge until the new house

was habitable. I felt grieved beyond measure—for the house and my mother, and I ached with tiredness and sadness. It was then that I picked up a book from a pile I had salvaged and brought from the house; it was a small book, rubbed with age: *The Meditations of the Emperor Marcus Aurelius Antoninus* and I opened it at that quotation: "Time is a stream in which there is no abiding."

Time Is a Stream

Eunice, her daughter, had a way of quoting, "If it were done when 'tis done then 'twere well it were done quickly," but not, Mrs. Throckmorton noticed, if it were Eunice who had to do it. Old Mrs. Throckmorton had always disliked the quotation —to her it sounded like a quip, and she disliked all quips—but for Eunice to say it now was cruel. The only possible way to do this—Eunice would have called it a "business" but to old Mrs. Throckmorton it was a breaking, a tearing apart—the only way for her was to do it slowly, so that the tear could be made little by little and the living tissue be given time to heal itself. Mrs. Throckmorton's lips were firm and disagreeable, but her soul was rocked and shrank and trembled.

Standing in the drawing-room where the packing-cases were already full, she touched, with a finger, the peacock feather fan that Eunice had taken out of the cabinet, with other things that had to be sold. The fan should have stayed in the cabinet where its colour had remained rich and brilliantly tender for years; "Years that the locust hath eaten but they hath not eaten the feathers," said Mrs. Throckmorton.

"Locusts can't be figurative *and* actual," said Eunice in her crisp, sure young voice.

Eunice was sensible, ruthlessly sensible. You could be ruth-lessly sensible, Mrs. Throckmorton thought, if you had a short nose; with a long nose it was not endearing. Eunice's nose was slightly long: it was the Dunbar nose. Mrs. Throckmorton's mother-in-law had been a Dunbar and Eunice was a thorough Dunbar. Sometimes Mrs. Throckmorton could not help wish-ing that Damaris had been able to come, or the more gentle Anne, but Eunice had no children and, of course, was such an excellent manager; she managed her husband (whom Mrs. Throckmorton often thought of as poor Tom), so that she was always free to get away. Eunice was to take Mrs. Throckmor-ton to the hotel in London and stay with her for a few days and find somewhere for her to settle. Mrs. Throckmorton sighed.

The fan had been brought back from India? China? Java? Anyway, from far jungles where the peacock had flown alive and wild; now it was transmuted into a fan and the fan had outlasted the peacock. Uncle McLeod had brought it home. "Your Great-Uncle McLeod, the boy in the painting by Ben-jamin West, with the white frilled trousers, holding the hoop. Where *is* the Benjamin West?"

"Packed," said Eunice. She hid a little yawn as she pushed in the straw of the last big case. "This will be all to go tomor-row," she said.

Mrs. Throckmorton did not see Uncle McLeod in the pic-ture; she saw him in the dining-room chair where he had sat when she was first brought in to shake hands with him; his head was bent, the creases of his chin went into his cravat. "Cravat? I must be very old," said Mrs. Throckmorton, but it was a cravat. The cravat was white too, but glossy, the chin full and flesh pink, the pink of an Ophelia rose. She saw him clearly; he seemed far more alive than Eunice with her neat mouse-coloured head, clear blue eyes and quick clearing-away hands. Mrs. Throckmorton drew a feather with its deep eye slowly through her fingers; the eye stared up at her. She sighed and put the fan back in the cabinet.

"Mother, you have put that fan away *again*."

"Yes, Eunice."

"As fast as I sort things out, you muddle them up again. You know all the things in the cabinet are to be sold. You can't keep everything."

"No," said Mrs. Throckmorton slowly.

"You will be far more free," argued Eunice.

"I do not wish to be free," said Mrs. Throckmorton in her voice that still was as deep as a bell, an old wether's bell leading a flock of obstinate sheep, old people who clung to old ways and old things.

"You know very well . . ." began Eunice, but Mrs. Throckmorton interrupted her.

"One does not wish to be free of one's house," said Mrs. Throckmorton in her bell voice, "not even in this generation."

It was a great house. Its windows reflected the day, as they reflected morning and evening, the passing of night and sunrise and sunset, through panes where the light, filtered green from the elms, fell on the floor and washed the walls; through the panes you looked out at the elms, the fields and flocks and quiet grey walls. In front of the house was a ha-ha; she remembered writing that to her mother in her first letter from the house. What is a ha-ha? A sunk fence with a ditch to separate lawns from fields. "Our parkland is green fields," she had written to her mother, "with elms and chestnut trees." There were nuts too in the lanes; at night the moon and the smell of country rose over the fields; a white cat gone hunting slunk by the new-mown hay; there were white lilacs in the garden and a magnolia up the wall. At first she had not liked the magnolia. "Why not, my love?" That was Eustace. "They seem—to eat the house." Then Eustace had spoken of the grace of magnolias in the Japanese painting in the study and she had objected. "Japanese painters etherealize. These are real," but she had grown to like the magnolias which now touched the roof. The chimneys were tall, clear, and strong, and their smoke rose, giving a message of reassurance to the neighbourhood. "We look to the big house." "Once," said Mrs. Throckmorton. "Once. Not now." The swallows flew back and built under the eaves of the house every year. The house would not change— for the swallows.

"Mother. You are looking white. You should go and lie down." Eunice opened the cabinet door to take out the fan.

"Eunice, I beg of you, leave that fan where it is. For today."

"Why not get it done?" asked Eunice sensibly. She laid her hand, not unkindly, but firmly, on her mother's shoulder; through the grey dress she could feel how its bones were hunched and bent; they increased her firmness. "You must accept, dear Mother."

"I do." Mrs. Throckmorton's voice could be harsh as well as deep, disagreeable to hear. Eunice winced but she stroked her mother's shoulder. They were nearer, in that moment, than they had been all this time; the older woman seemed to sink and sway as if an eddy had caught her under her daughter's hand. "I do," she said as if she gasped, and then she seemed to come up for breath; "I do, but you can't expect me to . . ." Enjoy it, she had meant to say, but what she said was, "endure it."

"Well then, as we have to have it out, let's have this tooth out quickly." Eunice sprang away and her voice was gay as if this determination were refreshing, but Mrs. Throckmorton refused to be refreshed. "It is not a tooth," she said. "It is a house."

"Oh, Mother!" said Eunice, irritated, "We know all that. Do you think we haven't felt it? We know it had to be done. Then do it. 'If it were done when 'tis done . . .'"

"Eunice!" Mrs. Throckmorton thundered. Then her voice broke. She was silent, trembling. At last she said, "I will not have these quips thrown at my head."

"It may be a quip but it's true."

"If I wanted to use words," said Mrs. Throckmorton bitterly, "I should find something as true . . . True but not wounding."

"Then what?"

"There are—other quotations."

"Name one," said Eunice triumphantly. She knew, and Mrs. Throckmorton knew that she knew, that her mother's weakness was that she was vague; even for Eustace Mrs. Throckmorton had not been able to achieve accuracy and clarity in the clear-tongued, clear-eyed, clear-brained way he had given to the girls. Stace, young Eustace, was the same as I, she thought; he understood, but Stace was dead, dead at Dunkirk. He had known what she could not explain, that, in her misty groping slowness, she was nearer to the truth; yes, Stace was the most truthful of her children. Tears pricked the thin lids of her eyes. How could she be clear when she dreaded this clearness? She was too riddled—muddled, Eunice, Eustace, and the girls would have said—but riddled was more true:

riddled with experience and facts and thoughts, truth, half-truth, light, half-light, whispered, caught illusions, dreadful shouted words. How do they expect me to be clear? I know too much, thought old Mrs. Throckmorton.

From where she stood, she could hear the rooks; the first Eustace and McLeod had heard them in their frocks; then generations of Eustaces and McLeods; it was the third Eustace who married a Dunbar and handed on her nose. Mrs. Throckmorton's own Eustace and their son and daughters, Stace, Eunice, Damaris, and Anne in their turn, had stood at the nursery window to watch the swallows come back, the rooks build again. We used to eat rook pie, thought Mrs. Throckmorton and she traced the edge of the cabinet, its inlay of scrolls and winding vines of leaves, with her finger. Only the backs, of course. You only eat the backs of rooks. She looked up and caught her daughter's eye. The rooks meant little to the girls. Eunice was smiling. "Name one quotation," challenged Eunice.

Something seemed to snap in Mrs. Throckmorton's eyes. Eunice saw that suddenly her mother's eyes were clear; usually, to Eunice, they looked slow, clouded, saurian, ugly eyes. Mrs. Throckmorton looked at the bookcase, walked straight across to it and took out a book. It was a small, rubbed-leather volume, one of four. She looked at the title: *Sayings of Marcus Aurelius*. That conveyed nothing to her but she opened it and ran her fingers down the page and stopped.

"Well? What is it?" asked Eunice. She was impressed.

The words looked up at old Mrs. Throckmorton from the page, and if the quip had stung her, these cut.

"Well? Read it," said Eunice.

Mrs. Throckmorton read in a whisper, " 'Time is a stream in which there is no abiding.' " The wound had wounded her. She was wounded by her own wound.

"But . . . How beautiful! How strange!" said Eunice in a changed, quiet voice. " 'Time is a stream in which there is no abiding.' But—it fits!"

"It fits," said her mother harshly and she threw off her daughter's arm.

Like water seeping through the floors, through cracks in the walls, through small holes and chinks, it had come; the first war; then, when Eustace died, selling off the land bit by bit to pay . . . the girls married and gone to their new homes: the second war: and Stace: and all the time, money grown less and less, repairs left over, costs rising. "You will have to give it up, Mother."

"I will never give it up."

"It's ridiculous, your living there all alone in that huge house. Mother, you must! Soon you will be reduced to absolute want."

"How can you be reduced to want if you don't want anything? I can live on nothing."

"No one can live on nothing."

"I have fruit and vegetables, I have the bees. I intend to sell the car and buy a goat. There is all this grazing. The rents pay for the rates and taxes."

"You need lighting . . ."

"I shall go to bed with the sun. I can gather wood for firing."

"The house is tumbling down over your head . . ."

"It will last my time."

"There are still things. Toothpaste . . ."

"I have no teeth."

Then her body had betrayed her, her old, ugly, Judas body. It had begun, for no reason, to faint. The first time it happened she had warned herself that it would be the end, did it ever show. It was bound to show; it seemed it was outside her power. Grudgingly she had to admit to it; her body fainted. "But what if it does?" said old Mrs. Throckmorton fiercely. She remembered a performing troupe she and Eustace had once travelled out with. Out where? It did not matter: Las Palmas, Bermuda, or Peru. They had been Japanese acrobats, a family, and they practised their thick-set contortions on deck every day. The mother had fits; if she had a fit they would place her by and ignore her, and when it was over, she would go on practising again. "That is the way it should be," said Mrs. Throckmorton, but the girls, Eunice and Damaris and Anne, did not think so; one of them, it seemed, would be impelled to give up her home and come and live with her unless . . .

It had, of course, to be "unless." The house was up for sale; they had all taken their pieces and tomorrow the removal van would come and remove Mrs. Throckmorton and her flotsam and jetsam, for flotsam and jetsam it had become, to a flat near Eunice. "Would you like a flat or rooms, Mother?"

"I do not care." Do not expect me, said Mrs. Throckmorton's look, ever to care again.

"Mother, be sensible. You know you cannot do with the house now. No one could do with it."

Now, in this time, it seemed people could not be wide; could not have a vision of the scope of quiet, of spaciousness. The lawns fell wide from the terrace to the ha-ha; in the elms the rooks had been for centuries as famous as the steeple of the ample Norman church. Here were rooms built for room, and corridors for pacing, and windows that ran from sill to ceiling and gave vistas of the land and cloud and sky. How beautifully light fell through the old Venetian blinds, slatted light and shadow on the floors, and light poured down the wall from the cupola over the stairs, touching polished wood and inlay, glass and paint, the flowers and flutings of china and rich patterns in the colours of the Persian rugs. "No, we were not afraid of living in our house then." But now family portraits, family Bible, family name were out of date; its seed was ploughed down in the furrow, and suffering took the young flesh as it took the wrinkles of the old. "It is not their fault but I judge them," said Mrs. Throckmorton harshly. She was not angry with them but with the cruelty of time; she felt a passion against the power of this flood, at its wanton drowning cruelty. She felt hate and passionate rage. "Let it come," said old Mrs. Throckmorton, but when it came it was not easy.

If only she could have been alone. Eunice brought her a cup of tea in bed and looked at her to see if she had slept. "Did you expect me to sleep?" asked Mrs. Throckmorton. Eunice waited near her all day, and all through the county, in the small town and the villages, in farms and cottages bright now with autumn flowers, michaelmas daisies, dahlias, golden-rod, in shops where they gossiped, they waited too, and as the tearing began, they felt for her and would not let her feel alone. The fibres gave up their clasp one by one, filaments with the minutes, and the minutes wrecked their way with the hours, as they waited round her. "Mother, are you all right?" "Sit down, ma'am, you oughtn't to be standing." "I called in, Mrs. Throckmorton . . ."

Twice she gave way, went under: once when a man she had

not seen before, a little man in a pepper-and-salt suit, whom Eunice said was an "expert," busy taking a magnifying glass out of his pocket and holding it over chair arms and table legs and frames and china, put it down on the mantel and rang one of her blue-and-white bowls with his finger and thumb. "But— I understood it was for sale, Madam," said the little man furiously. "Not today. Today it is a private bowl." "Oh, Mother! Come away." Once was when she came on the spice cabinet standing outside on the white sand of the kitchen path. For a moment she had failed to understand. She stood looking at it, holding to a piece of ivy from the wall. "But you said it should go with you, Mother." "It shouldn't go anywhere," said Mrs. Throckmorton in an ugly loud voice. "It belongs. It belongs on the wall in the kitchen between the clock and the dresser. You know that very well. It is not an ornament. It is for spice. Where else should it go?" "Mother, listen." "I will not listen. These are facts," and as she said that, a dark young man in a green apron, green and dark as the ivy, came up and gave her a look of pity and picked up the spice cabinet and carried it away.

When sunset came they were closing up the back of the van. It seemed to Mrs. Throckmorton to be a white sunset, without colours, richness, or promise, sterile. The rooks cawed but no smoke went up from the chimneys. Eunice fetched her mother's bag and gloves. "Shall we go?"

"Yes. No," said Mrs. Throckmorton.

"Do you want to go through the house again?"

"Yes." With the white light on her forehead, Mrs. Throckmorton went through the rooms. The last thing she saw was the nursery fireguard with a label on it, a white label printed with the figure 50; it was standing at the foot of the stairs in the hall; it had a hole in it where Stace had kicked it through. A strand of pale blue wool was threaded through the wire. Mrs. Throckmorton bent down to pull it, but then left it and walked away. Her heels made an insignificant tapping noise on the bare floors, but she put her hat straight and went out of the front door, touched the knocker with her gloved hand, and walked down the drive to where Eunice was waiting with the car. They drove away, not on a road, thought Mrs. Throckmorton, but on a swift cruel tide.

The girls had chosen an expensive luxury hotel. "A complete change for Mother. Something utterly different. It will help her to forget." They had settled that in their clear-sighted way. Now Mrs. Throckmorton stood, tall, in the foyer, waiting while Eunice registered and got their keys. The lights were bright, a throng of people passed through and in and out of the turning glass doors; telephones rang, lifts sang up and down and small page boys in coffee-coloured uniforms, with pert white gloves, went through the crowd, calling out names for messages. Mrs. Throckmorton, her hat slightly on one side again, faced an urn filled with gladioli, golden-rod, and orchids.

"Isn't this rather fun?" asked Eunice, her face flushed, coming across and taking her arm.

"They do not mix," said Mrs. Throckmorton.

"What don't mix?"

"Orchids and golden-rod." She nodded towards the urn. Then she shut her eyes. "Let the—the dénouement—be swift." She did not like "dénouement," not French words; then use an English one. "The end." Her skirt was bagging at the knees; she had wisps of hair on her neck, her hat was sliding, her face felt dark and raw. "You shouldn't have brought me here," she said to Eunice.

"Oh, come, Mother. It will cheer you up. You will feel quite different after a hot bath. We each have a private bath. Isn't that splended?"

"Splendid. Sumptuous," said Mrs. Throckmorton in her loudest bell-wether voice.

The bathroom was sumptuous, white, tiled and vast, with chromium fittings. "Rather different," said Eunice, "from home with that old mahogany-edged tub and the chipped willow pattern. Perhaps they will put basins in now." The bathroom lights were also bright; they made Mrs. Throckmorton's body in the bath look more than ever ugly and wooden and worn; like the body of those wooden Christs you see in the roadside shrines abroad; weathered by all weathers, stark. For the first time, she thought, she saw herself stark naked.

In the hotel dining-room there was a press and a clatter of tongues and silver and china and glass; she was too tired for the hotel dining-room; she could neither eat nor talk but sat upright and criticized the wine and sent the soup away; the waiter who took it had derision in his eyes for this old woman, opinionated, ugly, harsh, and slow, this old—the waiter would not think of Christ for a woman—this old fakir of a woman, bound to an idea. The idea of a house, thought Mrs. Throckmorton slowly, turning her glass with the second order of wine (Eunice was being wonderfully patient). A house is more than a building in which to dwell, a dwelling place or an inn; it is more than household affairs; it is a family, kindred, a line; it is genesis, the sign, to men among men, of a living force, of life. Life as you do not know it, said Mrs. Throckmorton silently to Eunice, to the waiter, to the crowded room. A house is a root and it is the root that bears the seed. That is what I believe, said Mrs. Throckmorton, and I am not wrong. When the waiter turned back again and showed them his face, his eyes were bland, and Mrs. Throckmorton despised him more than ever.

"Are you enjoying it, Mother?"

"No, thank you, Eunice. I am too old."

"You are tired. Soon you will be in bed."

In bed was no use. No rest. There were no trees outside the window, no field sounds, no gentle air; even with the window open the room smelled of central heating and the press of bodies, and the sounds were the sounds of lifts and bells and, far off, the streets below. The sheets on the bed had turned a faint grey with quick laundering, the pillows were unfamiliar, the satin eiderdowns oppressive; she wanted the old red paisley folded at the foot of her bed, light and warm on her feet, the thin linen case on her pillow, and to wake for a moment at dawn and hear the cocks crow from the farms, the wind rustle the elms, and to sleep again till the morning. A rush of regret filled her, not regret of pathos but furious regret. Why did I do it? Why did I let them make me do it? I should have consented to die first, frozen to death or starved. Her cheek felt like a cinder against the pillow, her eyes were gritty and hard. Let me die now, said Mrs. Throckmorton, but she went on living, her heart beating steadily in the dark hotel. She could not bear it. She put on the light. She woke Eunice in the next room and Eunice came in.

"Not sleeping, Mother?"

"Do you expect me to sleep?" she said tartly, for the second time, and she asked, "What were those words I read to you that morning?"

"Yesterday?" Eunice asked sleepily.

"Was that yesterday? Yes. Those words I liked."

"You didn't like them. They made you angry."

Mrs. Throckmorton brushed her hand across the sheet impatiently. "Say them."

Eunice said, slowly because she was sleepy, "Time—is a stream—aaah!—in which there is no abiding."

"No abiding," said Mrs. Throckmorton. "You are sure? Sure those were the words?"

"Quite sure," said Eunice, more awake, "Time is a stream in which there is no abiding." She looked at Mrs. Throckmorton and thought she looked very frail. "I shouldn't think of it now, Mother."

"No abiding," said Mrs. Throckmorton on the hotel pillows. "No abiding." She looked round the hotel room. "That is the healing—in the end . . ." She shut her eyes. "Go back to sleep, Eunice. I am very glad."

❦